Cinderella Effect

Nothing Here is Forever

By
Vaishnavi MacDonald

Published by Pen It! Publications, LLC in the U.S.A.
812-371-4128 www.penitpublications.com

ISBN: 978-1-954004-50-4
Edited by Rachel Hale & Dina Husseini
Cover Design by Sanghamitra Dasgupta

Nothing here is forever…

A ray of hope, a warmth of comfort, for the forlorn and cold though belonging to the cinders.

Learning to love and hope against all odds & overcoming the fear that hinders.

Then it is shattered, and all of the hope lost, burning the cinders again all over.

All the beauty and love gone, accept your fate 'Cinderella', for nothing here is forever....

I dedicate this book to my dear husband, Leslie, and my daughter Maggie, whom God has blessed me with.

Table of Contents

Chapter 1

It was a cool autumn morning. There was a piercing chill in the air today as it was windy. Ann was jogging it out to feel warmer. She had first decided she would brisk walk, but it was too cold today for comfort despite her warm jacket and warm woolen track pants on. She jogged past the lane that led to her neighborhood down a mile from there.

She lived in Orange County, California with her Hispanic adoptive parents, Cristian and Elena Gomez. Her full name was Ananya Gomez, previously O'Connor, but that is to be a long story. She was from India by origin, called Ann for short by her family and friends. Ann wasn't very tall. Just a good average for an Indian girl, 5'6". She wasn't very fair either but had a golden beige complexion and a great skin texture. She had thick dark brown wavy hair that had been cut into soft bangs that gave her oval face a little body, but she preferred them tied in a ponytail during work and exercise time. She had mixed Indian features with those almond-shaped hazel eyes so typical of the south Indian side, where her biological mother Sukanya hailed from. The other half of her exotic looks came from her biological father's side, who was from the Sind Punjab region of India. She had a slim but curvaceous frame and would take much care to remain on the slimmer side by regularly exercising and following a vegan diet.

She loved watching Hollywood. But was also very fond of Bollywood movies and songs though she understood very little of the language because she was bought to the United States by her mother at the age of six years. By profession, she was a youth counselor in her community social service team and very efficient in her job, especially with sexually abused or drug-addicted young girls. She spiritually believed in God but wasn't religious. Well, does that sound picture perfect to you? Wait 'till you read further.

As she jogged with just her one ear pod on, listening to some old classic songs, she suddenly heard a shrill piercing scream and then a muffled sound of a girl from a nearby warehouse kind of place with no other residential house half a mile on both sides of it. The neighborhood at this hour of the morning when it was still dark, as it was 5:30 am, was almost secluded and pin-drop silent. She felt a shiver go down her spine.

For the last two years, the drug and crime scene with youngsters had increased near their vicinity alarmingly. There was recent news of a certain gang of drug peddlers and drug lords whom Ann and her team had been up against in the past, who were once again targeting young teenage kids in the vicinity and one minor girl, Clara Smith, was kidnapped two weeks before this. She had been introduced to drugs near her school area and Ann was given her to counsel. The social service that Ann worked for was called Love, Life, Light Center for the Youth and Young Adults. This social service team at times worked closely with the cops in rescue operations of the youngsters caught up in drug rackets and the flesh trade of minors. Down the years, Ann had been passionately involved in the rescue cases of a dozen youngsters from either drug addiction or sexual abuse within the family and a few human trafficking cases too. This not only made her kind of a hero with the local people and the cops but also got her a bunch of enemies from the wrong side.

Right now, too, after hearing that scream, Ananya feared whether any girl was in trouble out there. She just walked swiftly but silently towards the source of the scream from the warehouse building. She had seen this place many times on her daily walks but never gave it much thought before this day. Wish she had her licensed gun with her. But whoever would carry one on a morning walk or jog. She had beads of sweat running down her temple despite the chill. She could see a broken windowpane amongst others on the worn-out part of the structure and decided to peep in quietly. With bated breath, she tiptoed to the broken windowpane and very slowly looked into the dark interiors from the corner when suddenly she heard something move behind her and before she could register anything she felt a sharp pain in the back of her head as if hit by a solid object.

"Aaargh …" was all she heard herself shout before she saw the stars in the daylight, lost consciousness, and fell on the ground.

Ann all of a sudden found herself in a dark, very scary, dense forest area. It was silent on all sides. Suddenly there was this figure that came out from inside the dark shadows around. The figure had a black robe and hood on. As he walked slowly towards her she was sweating profusely, and her heart was racing like a hamster on a roller. She was moving backwards gulping for air as her throat became dry like a parched land. The darkness became a thick wall behind her. She couldn't go back anymore when the hooded figure closed in on her. As he reached in front of her, her face was down with fear as she didn't want to look at him. When she slowly did look up, shaking badly, the hooded guy had a strange mask on, and he slowly lifted it off. And whom she saw behind it left her speechless. It was her stepfather Kevin O'Connor standing with a wicked smile on his face as he lifted his hands towards her face and she screamed loudly, "Noooooo ...don't... don't touch...me!"

When she gained consciousness, Ann was shouting exactly those words from her mouth in a softer tone compared to her nightmare. Once conscious, she realized she was in the familiar surroundings of the city square hospital where she had been a regular down the years with the complications some of the youngsters in their social service team would run into health-wise. But now the difference was that she was on the hospital bed. They had put a small bandage on the back of her head, she could feel it as she lifted her hand to touch the spot on her head where there was this throbbing pain. She realized thankfully it wasn't a major blow, but they had given her sedatives, so she still felt lethargic. All of a sudden, she heard a strong voice stop her from the other side of the room she hadn't noticed.

"Stop...don't touch that one. Relax."

She looked towards the glass windowpane of the room. He was standing there this tall, almost 6 feet, tanned skin American man with a strong jawline and a rugged personality you wouldn't exactly call conventionally handsome. As he walked towards her bed, Ann realized he had this uncanny attractiveness that was instantly noticeable. *He must be around 35 years old*, Ann guessed. She had never seen him before. He was wearing worn-out blue jeans and a red checker t-shirt with roper boots on. Looked quite western in his style and he probably was. As he came closer, Ann saw the deepest and sinister bluish-green eyes she had ever seen in her twenty-eight years on the planet. It unsettled her more than she could take.

Time to get into your shell Ann, no matter whoever this is... Her mind told her as it always did when she met some unknown person, especially from the opposite sex.

"Well, may I ask who you are...Mr.....?" she questioned.

He looked at her without a smile and stretched his hand out. "I am Phil McKay, from Nevada. I recently came down to Orange County and I happened to be in the neighborhood where you were hit by some mysterious guy who managed to get away while I helped to get you to the hospital. How are you feeling now?"

Ann didn't give the handshake back. She was still unnerved from the nightmare and her guard was on even as she stole her glance away from him, and looking down self-consciously, she asked, "Thank you for your help, but what were you doing there so early in the morning may I ask?" she couldn't trust anyone, especially this stranger.

She saw Phil's jaws clenching a bit as she stole a glance at him.

"I was trying to locate my... err... missing fiancée ... we had a tiff when she left Nevada...she came down to meet a friend here in the same locality in Orange County last week. Her cell is also switched off," he said without any emotion.

Ann now looked up surprised. Almost spontaneously she replied, "I...I heard a scream of a girl in that warehouse that's why I went there to check... did you see anything ...see ... hear any girl.. anyone?"

Phil looked amused she thought. "No, I didn't notice anyone else there. The man who hit you had a hooded jacket and a strange mask on so I couldn't see his face and he ran off alone. The cops of course must have covered the area by now."

A strange mask on? That rang a bell in her mind, but she brushed it off as a coincidence.

"Ho...how did...you... get me here?" Ann asked curiously.

"You were knocked out. I had seen the hospital nearby so I just put you into my vehicle and got you here. I informed the cops in the meantime. They will be here any moment."

Suddenly the familiar face of the middle-aged Afro-American nurse, Lara Brown, peeped in and looked at Ann with mock anger. She belonged to the same church community as Ann.

"Girl…rest if you wanna be on your feet and up to help those gals of yours. You can meet ya new boyfriend later…and you are Mr. …?" she asked the last words looking straight at Phil with a naughty smile. Lara was a pleasant-looking, chirpy middle-aged lady, with a medium built and a forever smiling face. Ann was fond of her and felt comfortable with her around. But there was one glitch, Lara wanted to see Ann settle down with a family of her own. And down the years she had been waiting for Ann to break out of her fears from the past and move on with a life partner which of course had been in vain to date.

Ann was aghast, "Hey now, no Lara …He…he is just someone who helped bring me here…" Ann tried to explain with blushing embarrassment, but before she could complete her sentence Lara blabbered away.

"Okay okay…No problem…thanks Mr. what did ya say your name is? Oh, you haven't…let me tell ya she is a hard nut to crack. If you got this one, I would say you should be awarded…"

Phil was obviously getting bored and impatient with the conversation. "Well let me put this straight. She is **not** my girlfriend. She isn't even my type." He rolled his eyes as he proclaimed it with a bit of rudeness.

Ann raised her brow unconsciously. What did he mean by that? She had never dated any men in the real sense. Not that she didn't try on persistence from the people around her, but the rendezvous always turned into a disaster. She just couldn't bring herself to be comfortable with a man or trust one, leave alone an American man, who would consider her way too conservative in normal circumstances too. She was bought up with Biblical values by her adoptive parents, the Gomez's. Not that quite a few from her church community itself had expressed their desire to woo her interest but they were mostly Hispanics, a few Indo Americans, and a few white Americans too, who were as conservative themselves.

He continued rather curtly, "I was just helping her on human grounds. I will wait for the cops outside," he said plainly and walked out.

Lara was shocked. She turned guiltily towards Ann and said with her cute accent, "Owww…so sorry mah dear, I was in an emergency meeting with Dr. Cliff regarding a scheduled operation when they got ya here... I …just I was so excited that ya finally…anyway he wasn't so bad to imagine you with... and I got ya cell phone from Nurse Rachel and ya parents called from San Francisco. I told them everything. They gonna be driving back today."

Ananya replied with despair, "No, please…don't tell me. I didn't want that. It's their holiday time together after ages. Dad finished his work there two days back and they are on vacation for a week nearby there…just give me the phone. I will tell them I am fine."

Lara looked like she again stumbled against a stone. She quietly gave Ann the cell. Ann dialed and waited for the ring tone.

****

Outside the room, in the hospital lobby, Phil sat looking at a giggly young girl on her cell phone, probably chatting with her crush in a hush-hush tone while some relative must be struggling for life inside. He couldn't relate to these silly emotions stirred by ever-changing hormones. *What's with these youngsters?* he thought. How short-lived are these attractions? Love, at first sight, was the crappiest thing ever. It was always lust. He once fell in love at first with this girl in high school, Maria Westerly. It was so intense for him, but she soon got over it like changing a pair of shoes. That was it. He had decided since then no woman would have the right to play with his heart again. He will always be the one in control of his emotions in a relationship. Other incidents of his life had made him even harder in his decision to keep away from the mushy stuff meant for sissy women when it came to romance. That's the reason he preferred women strong enough to stand up with him, also independent in their thinking.

His thoughts broke when he saw two cops come walking towards that part of the hospital corridor. One older and the other much younger. They looked at him as he stood up.

"Phil McKay," he said shaking hands with them.

"Oh yeah...Officer Harry William's and this is my junior officer, Matt Johnson. Thanks, Mr. McKay, for informing us about the attack on Ms. Gomez," said officer Harry.

"Just my duty as a citizen, officer. Well, I am from Nevada. I have been in town for just one day. I am here to see my fiancée Judy Martinez who was down visiting a friend in Orange County last week," Phil said, again without much emotion.

The younger cop, Matt Johnson, a good looking Hispanic around thirty years old, looked a bit impatient and said, "Okay. We are here to question you and Ann…err…I mean Ms. Gomez regarding the attack on her this morning." The younger man almost blushed, thought Phil.

Phil with a twitched smile said, "Sure. But let me tell ya, I know nothing much, just that as I was looking around to locate my fiancée in the same neighborhood I spotted this man hitting Ms. Gomez with a baseball bat from behind and he would have probably hit her again if I didn't shout loudly. He ran away almost immediately taking the bat with him. I didn't see his face because he had a hooded jacket on black denim material and a mask on his face. And then I had the choice either to get her here on time or chase him."

Officer Harry replied, "Of course, thank you so much, Mr. McKay. You did the right thing. We'll look into the rest. We will now see Ms. Gomez if she is ready."

Lara was prompt to reply as she heard them while coming out of Ann's room.

"She ain't gonna meet no one as of yet officer...the girl needs rest."

Officer Harry replied asserting, "Well, won't be much of a bother Nurse Lara. Duty calls. We'll need just five minutes so we can also relieve this gentleman."

He pointed to Phil. Lara looked almost doubtful of that credential since she found Phil McKay rather rude in their previous conversation concerning Ann. But she just shook her head and said, "Don't stay long," and walked away.

Officer Harry shook his head, "Well looks like they are the only ones doing their duty here I believe. And we, well, shall we go in?" he gestured humorously with his hand. Phil thought he was quite a jolly man for a cop.

Phil followed the officers into Ann's room. Ann was not on the bed. But in ten seconds she came out of the bathroom ready to leave, bandage and all. She had already changed her clothes at lightning speed after Nurse Lara left.

"So much for the 'let her rest'," Officer Harry said sarcastically under his breath as he continued, "Ms. Ananya Gomez, we just need five minutes girl. And we will be gone."

Ananya smiled, "Officer Harry, I will be gone before that. Well, I have no one to complain against and no confirmed suspects as usual...so?"

Officer Matt intervened, "Ann..."

Phil was surprised at the use of her first name by Matt.

"Why do you always have to be in such a hurry? This is for your good and your protection. Think clearly...there have been issues in the past too with these guys. And this time there has been an attack on you. I believe they are trying to target you, try to recollect, anyone, anything you saw today? This gentleman here says you were being attacked by a hooded guy from behind at that secluded warehouse. What were you doing at that abandoned place? Did you notice anyone there? Or have you ever seen Mr. Phil McKay before this around here..," he said looking suspiciously at Phil.

Phil was staring at her continuously in a very strange manner as if he was trying to scan her thoughts. Matt Johnson on the other hand knew Ann down the years as they attended the same college a year apart in grade. But he never got close and personal with her ever because she always had this unapproachable wall around her. Later she and her team would often associate with the local cops regarding the cases they handled in the social service team and that's the closest he ever came to her.

Officer Harry was quite fond of Ann, too, as he had a daughter close to her age. Matt Johnson was on the other hand smitten by her as his eyes were filled with a deep admiration towards her built not in a short while and not without reason. Ann knew the effect she had on Matt Johnson every time she was in the precinct for something related to the cases. And it would unnerve her. The problem was with Ann, who couldn't be alone with a man in a crowded place. She couldn't bring herself to trust a man to be in a romantic relationship ever. Not even a young good-looking officer like Matt Johnson. And now this Phil guy was affecting her in an even stranger way with those mysterious eyes of his.

"Well, I .... was walking around ...brisk walking actually. I heard the sound of a girl's scream from that warehouse...was just concerned.... thought I will check, what if anyone needed help?" She told them the truth. "Did your people find anything there?" She asked Officer Harry.

"Hmm, makes sense now. We found a USB speaker inside there without any pen drive in it. So, whoever knew you would be walking there purposely got you to come to him before hitting you. Might be the same people who threatened you in the past," said Officer Harry equally worried now since the possibility of such things happening was on the rise there.

Matt Johnson said looking straight at Ann, "Look I think you need to come to the precinct so we can discuss what needs to be done for your safety."

Ananya looked at Phil and then at Matt. Clearly, she wasn't comfortable with either of them staring at her. She could feel her palms sweating. Even as her throat turned dry. It was happening to her again, though after almost six months of her last panic attack when she was stuck in a lift failure in a shopping mall with a guy staring at her. Maybe today it was the head injury and the nightmare she had earlier that affected her right now she reasoned.

Before they could react, she grabbed her cell and bag from the bed saying, "Sorry Officer Harry, Matt, that was all there is to it. See you later. Thanks for everything. I have to visit a friend urgently."

And she ran at lightning speed out of the room, the corridor, the hospital lobby, and the main gate. The men stood like statues where they were, taken aback at what had just happened.

Chapter 2

Ananya put on the music in the car. Now she could relax as she drove her car towards San Jacinto. She had already spoken with her close friend Brittney to stay with her for a couple of days 'till her nerves settled down. She had also called up Nurse Lara and said sorry to her. Got a solid scolding from her but she was still so adorable.

Relationships, though few, were very important to Ann; more than the material things around and she took extra pain to keep them alive. Speaking of pain, there was still a throbbing pain at the back of her head getting a little severe as the pain killer began to wear off. She had taken the medicines along.

After she ran away from the hospital, she took a cab home and packed some stuff at a lightning speed and left the house in her car all in one breath. But in all the hurry, she left her cell phone at home. It was not advisable to turn back now. She was already twenty-five minutes on her way and didn't want to run into Officer Harry, or Matt, or the stranger Phil again. Matt Johnson would have called her to the precinct or come to her workplace and picked her brains so that he could spend some extra time with her. She decided she would get a new temporary cell number in San Jacinto. Better still, do without one for two days. It was a day to the weekend anyway. And she had somehow convinced her vacationing parents not to rush back to her.

Ann smiled to herself remembering in her teens how she would be silly enough when she would spot a group of boys and would rather take a longer route to avoid crossing their path. Things hadn't changed much in that context. She was still running away. She wondered what Officer Harry must think of her. She was kind of fond of him because he was the only other man apart from her adoptive father Cristian, who she knew would never think of her in any other way but fatherly. But Officer Harry knew very little of her past and not more than Matt Johnson did. The Gomez's had made sure to protect her in every way. The greatest irony of Ann's life was that she, a bachelor's in psychology and a qualified counselor, who counseled young girls so efficiently to overcome their problems couldn't overcome the fear of trusting a man too close to her. This was her secret known only to those very close to her and of course those few men who ever tried getting close to her. It is called Genophobia in technical terms and the fear of getting physical with a man in simpler terms. And a severe one in her case, despite taking help from various therapists.

The music playing on the deck in her car was an old country-western classic, 'Choices' by George Jones, that her adoptive father Cristian always put on while she went long-distance driving with them. She sang along with the lyrics, "*I have had choices since the day I was born, there were voices that told me right from wrong....*"

The song suddenly faded as her mind went back to her childhood memories. Some that had shaped the good part of her life today and others that were responsible for her biggest problem ever, her phobia problem. It came back in bits and pieces as flashbacks every time she was disturbed or sometimes, they would surface in the form of nightmares. Right now, her mind drifted off years back.

Flashback

"Mama, are we going to stay here forever with Uncle Kevin?" Asked the innocent six-year-old Ananya.

"Yes, my darling and he is no longer Uncle Kevin, it's Dad from now on. Your new daddy," Ananya's mother Sukanya made her understand softly.

"Mama, wow...my own daddy? That means Jaanvi had said I can't have a daddy ever."

Little Ananya innocently quoted her friend back in India.

Kevin O'Connor carried little Ananya into his arms and kissed her on the cheek, "Well dear, she didn't know I was going to be the knight in the shining armour did she," he joked looking at a happy Sukanya.

Sukanya, with little Ananya, landed in the United States of America three months earlier and they were now living in her new husband Kevin O'Connor's palatial estate in Los Angeles. He was quite a wealthy businessman and a very influential one, though quite older than Sukanya. He had several failed marriages and relationships before going into a relationship with the beautiful Sukanya Nair Kapoor, a widowed Indian who had a six-year-old daughter. Kevin and Sukanya had got married within two months of her coming to the USA. And all the legal formalities were already put in place by Kevin O'Connor beforehand.

Sukanya, a very soft-spoken and naive woman, had previously been married to Ananya's Punjabi father back in India for just a short while because sadly, she became widowed early when Ananya was barely two. She met Kevin O'Connor four years later when the Irish American businessman came to visit a foreign collaboration company in India where Sukanya worked as a personal assistant to the MD. They had an instant attraction because Kevin was such a lady charmer, and he found her challenging as she first resisted his flirtations. Then followed a torrid affair between them after which she decided to follow him to the USA when he asked her. Little Ann didn't exactly remember her real father's face or interacting with him except the pictures her mom showed her. She longed for a father's love and that's the reason she innocently took to Kevin as a father almost immediately.

****

Back to the present moment

Ananya jammed the emergency breaks as deep in those thoughts she didn't notice a huge goods trailer before her slow down. The driver gave her a dirty look through the side mirror before moving on. She sighed relief.

"Wake up, Ann. Stop it, at least while driving, don't go there. Be alert," she chided herself. Ann switched off the music on the deck. "Let's concentrate on the road," she told herself.

A little ahead she pulled over to a gas station to fill up. As the gas machine was doing its bit, she just looked around taking a whole turn. She suddenly noticed near a rocky patch on a small hill behind the station, someone standing half-hidden by a huge boulder. It was a black-robed hooded figure just like her stepfather in her nightmare earlier that morning. It looked like that person was staring right at her. But she couldn't see the face because of the distance and the hood. She panicked. It felt like her breath would stop just there.

"How can this be? Am I hallucinating? Am I losing it?" she asked herself. She had nightmares about this but now she was seeing it in real-time. The gas was full. She removed the hose and shut the tank. When she again looked back to the spot on the hill, there was no one there!

She quickly got into the car and drove off, screeching the tires in a hurry to get on the way. People around looked at her with surprise.

On the way again, Ann contemplated what she saw. In psychology, she had learned how past experiences can trigger hallucinations even years later. Because 'till now she only had recurrent nightmares but never a hallucination, ever. And then there was her mother's medical history of an unstable mind but that was circumstantial.

"No ...no. There wasn't anything there...just my imagination...I am not going to dwell on it... *'The perfect love of God casts out all fear'(1 John 4:8)."* She quoted her favorite Bible verse every time she was scared. It actually gave her renewed strength.

She just kept her eyes on the road and sped on. But seeing that robed and hooded figure took her back to the saddest part of her childhood memories yet again. The flashbacks from her past started to sweep across her mind like an old film reel in a projector she had no control over. This time they were the dark and violent ones.

Flashback

"Please Daddy, don't... hit Mummy...please. I... I will... listen to you...I...I.," sobbed seven and half-year-old Ananya pushing him away from her mother with her tiny hands.

All was initially fine for the first year of her mother, Sukanya, and Kevin O'Connor's marriage. Problems began when incidents of Kevin's infidelity began to rise. Since then, these daily fights had become commonplace in their home with her stepfather Kevin getting more violent by each day 'till things got worse.

Ann was so lost in her memories that she didn't notice someone was following her in a big black SUV. She, in fact, went from one morbid memory of her past to another.

Flashback

"Aaah…no…Daddy please…don't beat me…it…it hurts …I promise I will obey you and ….I will….no…please don't…aah…," the now eight and half-year-old Ann was crying out loudly in pain as Kevin O'Connor, heavy on leisure drugs, took out his anger on little Ann. Sukanya came to know too late that Kevin was actually a rising member of a secret occult group, a cult where he was involved in dark activities. So along with alcohol now, he would have some strange new-age drugs too that made him hyper and mad. But then being the sadist that he was in reality, he enjoyed beating Ann up more than Sukanya. That's when Sukanya came in between them and started getting brutally assaulted. Sukanya was fragile in her mental strength to bear all these things.

The violence started getting so ugly that the cops were alerted by a well-wishing doctor when he saw the assault marks on Sukanya. But Sue would refuse to press charges against Kevin on all those occasions as he had threatened to destroy Ann if she opened her mouth against him. The next thing Sukanya got to know was that the doctor had an accident that caused his death. Deep inside she felt this must also be related to Kevin somehow.

Many times, she begged him to send her back to India, but he refused because there was much more being planned in his evil mind. In fact, very soon Sue came to know that Kevin married her only because he had seen innocent Ananya and had an evil plan for her in the future. So, the ordeal continued, especially for Ann. Until the water went above the head eventually.

Here Ann stopped. Her eyes were moist. She got hold of her emotions. After another five minutes down the road, she was feeling a restless monotony setting in, so she put the music on in the car deck again. This time with her favorite Hindi travel song 'Mahi ve' from the Bollywood movie 'Highway'. She had learned the lyrics and their English translation too. They were kind of philosophical ones, about life's journey and its connection to a road trip. Her past life was also so close to the story of the heroine of that film, Ann felt; only darker and messier.

"But cheer up Ann, you have a lot to thank God for too," she pepped herself up as she did many times.

Ann looked into the rear mirror, loudly singing the lyrics of the song. She saw the black SUV behind her driving at her pace, so she sped up a bit. There weren't many vehicles on the road so suddenly the black SUV behind her zoomed next to hers, pushing her to the left edge of the border between the opposite side traffic. She was taken by surprise at this. Then the burly guy driving looked at her and gave a very sinister grin that unsettled her. While the thinner guy next to him chuckled. They both wore black suits. *Pretty decent for such psychopaths*, thought Ann. She didn't react but just pumped the accelerator and moved ahead. Her car was a manual one as it was a much older model. But she was attached to it and refused to part with it. Theirs was the latest model in SUVs. So, her car struggled to stay steady while they seemed to enjoy the race that went on for the next five minutes. She just slowed down and let them go ahead moving to the right again. Ann was paranoid about what might be their intentions. They suddenly went ahead, and Ann relaxed, they were no longer interested in her. But the fear they had bought in her got those flashbacks back again.

Flashback

"Come on baby girl…take it…. it's fine to take it…was it not good last time? Nothing happened. See…look at your mom. She feels so calm and peaceful after taking it. See…see…," Kevin, Ann's stepfather, was coaxing ten-year-old Ann to take one of those new-age drugs again as he also regularly gave them to her mother Sukanya, who by now had got addicted to them. Ann saw her mother lying limp on the couch unable to get up or help her. Sukanya had begun to slowly lose her mind when Kevin started to forcibly administer those strange drugs to little Ann as well and there was nothing she was able to do to stop him.

"No Daddy. This is …not good…I don't like it….my schoolteachers… tell us. We must not… take it… even… adults…sh… shouldn't….," she said with tears in her eyes, stammering out of fear as to how her stepdad would react.

"Ok, you disobedient wretch…you will not go to school now onwards. Homeschooling it is for you."

"No Daddy, please. I want to go to school and meet my friends…please."

Kevin smiled wickedly and gave the drugs to Ann who didn't resist this time. But school did stop for her eventually and homeschooling began. After all, Kevin's secrets; he wouldn't let them get out so easily.

****

Back again to the present moment

Ann was sweating profusely despite the car AC on full blast. She looked at the rear mirror. The black SUV was back again a little behind her now, and the guys were still on her case from the look on their faces. She felt like taking a right turn somewhere to lose them and then get back on the road. They were unsettling her nerves now. She saw a right turn a couple of yards ahead and move towards it swiftly slowing down as the SUV guys again went ahead of her in speed and then they also slowed down as if waiting for her to catch up. She immediately took the right turn as it came. It was a rough path in the countryside. She went a bit ahead and stopped with her heart beating fast.

"Let me wait for five minutes before I move back. They will have been gone far by then," she said to herself. As she sat there, her mind once again was lost.

Flashback

"Daddy, please Daddy, don't let them take Mummy away...please...Daddy...I will do what you tell me. Please...please!" little Ann cried loudly. She was eleven by now and already into the drug addiction Kevin had forced her into. Now Kevin could make her do anything he wanted as she had become like a slave to it and him. The concerned authorities were called by Kevin to take her mother to the center for mental health for the treatment of a severe onset of Schizophrenia and some other vague mental illness. Kevin made sure that it would be a long stay for her there.

It had been too much for Sukanya to take in when she got to know that Kevin had been involved in that dark secret cult of his years before they met in India. There were rituals performed and demonic orgies celebrated to please a demon god whom the cult worshipped. All this was to gain more success and power in the world. He had slowly started to force Sukanya to participate in the rituals that started taking place sometimes in their huge estate home at night when strange people came there and wore those black robes and hoods over their heads for the ritualistic ceremonies.

The last straw for Sukanya was when she overheard them talk with Kevin to offer the young Ananya as planned, as a sacrifice to their demon god. It was after that she mugged enough courage and decided to run away from there with little Ann and seek help, though she was mentally and physically very weak by then to do so. Ann remembered how desperately her mother had tried to get Ananya away from there, but her plan had failed. Kevin was too evil and cunning for her and a very influential man with connections in high places. And now he was very angry with Sukanya. He kept her locked in a room for four days even as eleven-year-old Ann was drugged and initiated into their evil cult rituals. Sukanya lost her mind and eventually, she was declared mentally incapable of living in normal surroundings.

As the young Ann pleaded with her stepfather Kevin not to let her mother be taken away, he smiled as he made her sit next to him. "Look, darling. I will get your mother back in just a week's time. You don't worry about that. But for that, you must promise Daddy that you will never disclose to anyone about whatever happens here or with you... Ever...Promise?" Kevin said with mock kindness, emphasizing on each word.

A petrified Ann nodded her head yes.

That's the day when Kevin made his first sexual advance towards her. He had waited 'till the first initiation of her into the rituals were over. This was all as planned in advance by him and a part of appeasing their dark demon god. Now, little Ann was left alone to the mercy of the equally demonic Kevin O'Connor.

At this point in her memories of her past, Ann's mind would go blank as if it didn't want to remember anything further about those unfortunate times of terrible damage caused to her psyche as a child. The disturbing flashbacks always ended at this point and would jump directly to the point of her rescue by the child welfare service.

****

Back to the present time

Ann looked in the rear-view mirror. Tears were streaming down her cheeks as she took a tissue from her bag and wiped her eyes and face. How many times she had done this she had lost count. She took a deep breath and gathered herself up and made a U-turn to move back towards the main road. As she joined the main road there were few vehicles on it and she smoothly got on her way relieved that those SUV guys were not in sight now.

She was a fairly good driver. Thanks to her adoptive parents, the Gomez's, who had installed this confidence in her down the years. They had given her a good education and value system too. Thank God she was rescued when she was, or she would have never met them. Almost a year later after being left alone with her stepfather, a child welfare team member alerted the authorities about something fishy happening at the O'Connor's estate, and Ann was finally rescued and questioned. With enough evidence against him from people around and seeing evidential proof in Ann's case, Kevin was given a long prison term on various charges. Ann had been sent to rehabilitation and counseling therapies.

Suddenly she was jolted out of her memories by a rude bang behind her car. The big SUV was again behind her and purposely banged her car and was now trying to overtake her in speed in order to take her off the road to stop her. *But why?* She wondered. She must have missed seeing them waiting for her when she was lost in her thoughts. They must know where she is going then. That thought made her go weak in her knees. She could see from the rear-view mirror they were trying to make her pullover at the side and stop her. She tried to speed ahead now, but their vehicle had more engine power compared to her old sedan and they caught up with her dangerously overtaking her and moving ahead of her car.

Before they could do anything further to her car, there emerged another SUV car from the back of a huge trailer a little far behind and came right behind Ann's car. It was a lighter SUV compared to the other one, but nevertheless, the driver seemed as crazy. She couldn't see his face through her mirror because he had a cowboy hat and huge shades on. He overtook her car in no time and even though she was fearful, Ann had this instinctive feeling that this guy was out there to help her because he immediately bought his hands out of the vehicle and gestured her to follow him. He slowed down and so did Ann behind him. The other guys were ahead of them. As the cowboy driver put the left indicator on, he gestured Ann with his hands to go to the left path off the road a little further down at a crossroad ahead. Ananya had only two choices, either detour behind him or else get caught up by the other SUV with those men looking out behind at her again and again. By instinct, she turned her car behind the 'cowboy's' vehicle without giving a second thought.

After a while, Ann felt the path never-ending as she kept driving aimlessly behind this stranger. The other guys surprisingly didn't come after them. Maybe they were just some miscreant revelers, she thought. She could see the pine woods on the hills at a distance indicating that her destination would have been very near the main highway. After driving for quite a distance on the rough narrow path they entered what seemed a thicket of pine trees and witch alder bushes along. Driving at speed without thinking much, now Ananya suddenly felt a shiver go up her hand and neck and goosebumps form on her skin. Who was she following without a single thought 'till now? What if he turned out to be one of those kinds and she had been tricked into following him? She hadn't even seen this man's face clearly because of the cowboy hat and shades. And why wasn't he stopping his vehicle either? They had long lost the miscreants. She was now with a total stranger in the secluded woods, alone! How she regretted forgetting her cell phone at home. If only she could call the cops or someone for help. Even the forever staring Matt Johnson would do at this point.

Chapter 3

Flashback

"She has gone through a lot, Mr. and Mrs. Gomez. Though we have sent her for a lot of therapy in her rehab, it's going to be a long battle. I warn you she is not going to be an easy kid to foster," the person from the child welfare system frankly told the childless Gomez couple when they readily accepted to foster Ann. They were strong believers in Jesus Christ.

When Elena Gomez heard Ann's full story, she could barely hold the tears in her eyes. Initially, Ann would squirm every time they tried to even look at her intently. All in all, she was a total mess when they got to foster her and they willingly chose her as they also had experience with similar cases before, being involved in the social service wing of their church. They decided eventually they would try for her adoption too, though having her mother still alive had posed the greatest challenge. But finally, due to Sukanya's uncertain mental conditions and after a long legal process, the Gomez's got to adopt Ann officially.

Ann felt warm and secure whenever she thought of the time the Gomez couple came into her life. They were the first ones to show her what a relationship with the loving God meant which she eventually, after turbulent teenage years and an equally disastrous onset of adulthood came to realize herself in her twenties. She had come a long way due to the spiritual strength she got but just that the phobia and panic attacks connected to it continued. But down the years she had learned to control and avoid every situation that led to those panic attacks in her and her best strategy was to just get away from the source immediately. And that's exactly what she was going to do even now, once again.

Ann saw a right path diverting ahead. As she saw the 'cowboy' guy drive straight on the path going uphill, she just swirled her car to the right, sure that there must a way out from there leading back to the main road. But after going quite a bit into the woods the track almost faded out leaving her in an open patch with nowhere to go. She decided to go back the way she came. She was so disturbed in her mind; she had lost her sense of direction. Suddenly as she tried turning the car around, she lost control of the steering wheel because of the unlevelled path of the hilly area, and the car got stuck in a small trench. She tried raising the accelerator hard, making so much noise in the silence of the woods, and then after some attempts, the car jerked out forward. But because she was so nervous, she kept her foot pressed on the accelerator instead of the brake and the car went down a slight slope in great speed and banged into a pine tree with the bonnet flying open before her. With that Ann was knocked out, more due to the shock of the impact, second time in one day.

Ann found herself in a different world suddenly and she saw her adoptive parents, the Gomez's, waving at her from a distance as she just floated in the air towards what seems a nice dewy place full of bright light, just like the description of heaven children are given.

"I have died and come to heaven. And they are saying goodbye to me," she sighed floating on a cloud.

Heaven was such an unbelievable place for Ann to imagine years back. For one she knew sin and evil had no place there. It must be a pure and holy dwelling of God and His pure souls.

And she always felt she was not good enough to go there because of the unholy things that had happened to her as a kid. She used to feel guilty for those unfortunate events. She would tell herself she had to become very good and pure to be allowed in God's abode. It took the Gomezs, who were more spiritual than religious, quite some years to convince her that it was never her fault whatever had happened to her. All she needed to do is believe God loves her so much that Jesus came and died for her. It took Ann her own pace to come to terms with this truth. And she eventually did.

Right now, she was mumbling a small prayer to God in her heavenly state, "God ...I know you love me a lot. Why else would I be allowed into heaven? But ... Where are you, Lord...I want to see you..."

"Right next to you ...," a familiar voice came to her ears loudly.

She opened her eyes with a startle at the voice and found her face and body compressed to the seat with the car safety airbag open. She looked at the driver's seat window and there he was again, bending over the car window, her 'hero' who had saved her this morning. Phil McKay looked on a bit sternly at her.

"Not a very nice way of thanking someone is it?"

Ananya could feel the heat rising to her cheeks even as she put her glance away from those disturbing eyes, but her face and body couldn't move at all. So, it was him again trying to help her. But why in the world was he going out of his way to do so?

"Ar... are you following me? I... how did you know I was on the way ...to San Jacinto?"

Phil looked a bit amused; she was stuck so funnily at this point and yet was questioning him.

"No, I didn't know. I saw two guys leave behind your car from outside your home in a black vehicle as you rushed out," he said getting her out free from behind the safety airbag. Once she was out, he asked, "Are you ok?"

Ann nodded her head in a yes, consciously aware she was alone with a relative stranger in the woods. She almost felt like red riding hood and he the bad wolf around her. He continued without noticing her discomfort, "Gotcha address from Officer Harry and I came to hand over this to you since you left so abruptly this morning. It fell out at the time of the attack. Thought it might be of importance to you."

He had her heart-shaped, 18-carat gold locket with her real mother and father's pictures in it. Too precious to lose and not because of the gold. Her adoptive parents gifted it to her and wanted her to have it as a remembrance of her roots. Some day she also wished to visit her birth country of India and her real parents' hometowns there.

She just grabbed the locket almost insolently and stepped back. She said slowly, not looking at him directly, "Thank you so much for...this...and ...also the morning and... now."

Phil had a slight grin as he saw her trying to avoid looking at him. He said, "Well thank me later. Let's first get you to a safe place. Where ever you were off to, those guys had your cell phone tapped, I guess. They know where you are headed for sure. You need to stay away in an unknown destination for a couple of days or maybe a week after this morning's attack."

Ananya was startled, "Wha...why....my friend Brit... I don't even have my cell...to tell her that…" Ann started sobbing, much to her own embarrassment. She continued, taking hold of herself immediately, "I am sorry. Just overwhelmed with all this. I don't exactly know who these guys are and why are they targeting me, though I have a hunch I think," she managed to finish her sentence without a break. They could be anyone, even revelers, though they were too focused on stopping her to be casual revelers or miscreants. For one they could be connected to the rescued girls and the drug peddler case her team dealt with.

"We can find out who and why...but let's get to a safe place and talk," Phil McKay said in a strange hurry as he took hold of her arm and gently pushed her to sit inside his SUV.

Ann tried getting herself free from his clutch as she panicked, sensing something not ok, but couldn't free herself as she said, "Let go Mr. McKay. I ...I don't want to know anything about anyone, and I want to just go to my friend's at San Jacinto. I'll take my car, thanks for everything."

Phil loosened his grip on her arm and looked towards her car which was still stuck near the tree with the bonnet open. It looked doubtful whether it will even start right now. Ann looked sheepishly back at him.

"Look let's not make it harder than it already is. Quietly come with me. You will be safer," Phil said a bit assertively now.

Ann was doubtful of the word 'safer'. Was it ever that? With a stranger of all people? She felt safe only in two places, one with her adoptive parents, the Gomez's, and the other with God, by herself.

She wasn't going anywhere with a strange man and his piercing blue...no green...no... whatever eyes. She strongly pulled herself out of his grip as she pushed him and ran towards her car. She thought she will lock herself in 'till he left and later walked it out for help to the main road to get the car towed. Phil was just taken by surprise a little, but before she could open the door of her car he rushed to her side and pushed her back to her car door. His face was now dangerously close to hers and his eyes were more blazing this time. She could feel his breath on her face. His hand had strongly pinned her to the car so she couldn't move a bit. Those piercing eyes tore into her soul. It was too much. She couldn't breathe. It was happening to her again, the panic attack, bringing flashbacks of the brutality with which her stepfather would treat her and her mother.... she shut her eyes tight not wanting to remember anything from that time right now. Suddenly she felt very weak in her legs and like a rag doll fainted right there in front of him.

This was unexpected for Phil. He had no choice but to just carry her in his arms and put her on the side of the driver's seat in his vehicle. He then took out the towing tool from the back of his vehicle and went to her car and attached it to his. He somehow was able to remove her car out from near the tree and then he drove off, going back through the path between the pine trees, this time uphill.

As he drove his vehicle, there were a thousand questions in Phil's mind. The answer was just one, Ananya Gomez. If only she could be a little stable around him. He knew all that he needed to know about her through sources. More than that, he wasn't interested in her. Just that he had noticed since that morning about the extent of her mental instability around men she was unfamiliar with. But whatever she had been through, he wasn't sure, she had not completely healed. It made him cringe because it bought back the memory of a person too dear to him.

There was something Ann didn't know about him though. That he had been following her this morning on her walk. Though he had no clue who had attacked her that morning, he wasn't surprised. Ann Gomez must be rubbing other people the wrong way too with her stubbornness. But those guys in the SUV had been planted by him a month back while he was still in Nevada, to follow her everywhere and give him all the information, and this morning he asked them to scare her and set her off track behind him. And of course, he had her phone tapped too, so he knew where she was heading. For Phil, Ananya Gomez was the only way to fulfill the life-consuming mission he was out for, in California!

Chapter 4

"Life doesn't spare you; circumstances don't seek to. But when You seek to love in all circumstances, then life spares you to seek it."

Phil shut the little diary he found in Ann's bag from her car after reading the first two pages filled with philosophical gibberish, he thought. He was disappointed as he expected to find much more in it. Some of the answers he wanted at least. Well, he would have to wait for her to come around he felt as he looked at her lying peacefully on the couch near the fireplace he had lit up. It was a small cottage well up the hills in the pine woods. He had the key to it as planned. It was quite remote. He was sure no one would find it. Not at least for the next few days. That would give him enough time to win Ann's trust or use force to get it out with, whichever. If only she would cooperate, things could go smoothly. He was so close to solving the puzzle and yet so far.

Phil had his math right but with Ann's unexpected behavior and constant fainting, he wasn't sure what could happen next. This was something he had not planned. He had handled all kinds of women in his thirty-six years of life. From a runaway mother in his childhood, to an unfaithful ex-wife of hardly a year-old marriage, to half a dozen attractive girlfriends with different personalities, to a much-loved younger sister...here, he stopped. He clenched both his jaws and his fist and hit it hard on the wooden table ahead of him. It made a loud sound in the quietness of the evening in the woods. That woke up Ann with a startle. She sat up and looked scared first trying to register where she was and then looked at him, angrily staring at the fireplace. His face was equally ablaze as the fire. She felt a fear sensation run through her neck area even as she mugged up the courage to ask,

"Hi...I... how long was I gone. I mean...an hour or more...?"

Phil didn't answer. He kept staring at the fire.

"I think it must have been ...been those sedatives in the...m... morning."

No response still.

"Look I know I should have listened to you. I g...guess you are right...this...this may be a safer place...I...," she finally said, thinking if she will be nice to him, he will at least not be cruel to her, whatever his intentions were of getting her here.

Instead, Phil just got up with anger and lifted her from the couch. Even as he held her close, he said indignantly, "Let's not beat around the bush. You know more than you would like to show. I need some answers from you and fast. Then I am gone. You won't see me again. Just make it easy for me, ok?"

Ann felt like she would suffocate if he held her any closer for long. "Mr. McKay plea...please let g... go of me or else I... I can't speak anything...,"

Phil realized she was almost turning blue. He let her go and turned his back to her and slowly apologized, "Sorry...I didn't mean to...,"

Ann gathered herself and went quickly towards the little open kitchen near the dining area pretending to be casual but more to get far away from him. She then started scurrying for some coffee powder as she needed some black coffee right away to calm her down and warm her up in the chill of the cottage. She could hear it rain outside. No wonder the fire wasn't enough to keep them warm.

Phil looked at her move, rubbing her arms and moving around, as if she were in her own space. Her black denim jacket was lying on the couch and she was still wearing the beige shirt with her favorite grey track pants of the morning. She could feel his gaze on her, and she wished the earth would just open and swallow her up. This was her big problem. All phobias can be treated she had learned as a counselor, but there seems to be no remedy to hers alone she felt as the damage hadn't healed in her soul yet.

She asked just to divert his attention, "I just want to have some coffee before we talk. I desperately need it. Isn't there any here?"

He picked up her jacket and quietly went to the kitchen area without answering her query and put the jacket on her shoulder. She immediately snuggled into it. That was better.

She said a low, "Thanks..."

No reply. He just opened a cabinet she hadn't noticed and took out a bottle of coffee. Just the brand she loved. He started to make the coffee himself as he took a kettle out and filled it with water. Ann was conscious of his every move as if he were a threat to her existence. She moved away quickly to the other side of where he stood near the electric stove.

Then she asked, "Well... I really can't comprehend what you may have to ask me but guess it's important to you."

He stopped for a second and continued saying, "It sure is. So much so if you don't give me the answers easily, I can keep you here for days or even.... months!"

Ann gulped. What was he wanting to know and what if she didn't know the answers? "Well, I will try to...but...what if I don't...know the ...answers..."

Phil stopped for a moment, then he suddenly turned to her with clear anger on his face as he came close to her and said, "You bloody hell know the answers. I know that for sure... only you have them."

Ann was shocked. Who was this man and why was everyone suddenly on her case? Ann tried to move away to a safer zone, but he stopped her as he pulled her close to his face and asked, "It's about Jade... Jade Jones...now does that ring a bell?"

Ann went cold in her feet. She felt she would faint again but this time she held herself strong as she always did when dealing with difficult cases of the youngsters as a counselor.

Jade...how could she forget her... her heart sank within her. It was more than one and half years from now and still so vivid. But why should she tell him about Jade? Who is he? Could he be him?? No. That guy had come and gone a year back. And she had made sure not to meet him or let him know about her. Why now? After so much gap. And that man's name was Phillip Jones, not Phil McKay. Wait a moment. Didn't Jade mention him as Phil in short? But the McKay still didn't match. *Oh, so confusing,* thought Ann.

As if Phil could read her mind, he said "I have been trying to solve the mystery for the last two years and it led me again and again to the source. You!"

Ann felt dizzy. It surely is him. He saw her body shaking badly and feared she would again faint, so he just picked her up without warning and bought her to the bedroom adjoining the hall. He put her down on the bed and said, "Relax...I am not gonna hurt you...lie down here while I get the coffee for you."

How could he be so rude and courteous at the same time? thought a confused Ann.

"Can I call my friend Brittney and tell her I am fine. Also, my parents generally talk to me at this time every day. They all will get suspicious and worried. If that's what you want?" she shouted loudly albeit with a shaky tone, so he could hear in the kitchen. Now she was using some psychological tactics here she thought. But Phil McKay was a 'Ph.D.' in psychology she got to know the next moment. He shouted back from the kitchen area, "Even they can't find us here. I made sure of that. I will give you the phone and your freedom both. Just tell me everything."

He bought the black coffee and gave her. She took it and said quietly. "Thank you."

He pulled a chair near the bed and sat on it next to her, again too close for comfort. Ann just squirmed away a bit towards the other side. Phil noticed it half amused. He wasn't interested in her of all the women on Earth. For one he preferred brave and independent women and secondly, they must be honest. That's where his ex-wife Sarah failed. When she cheated on him big time with one of his old buddies. And he wasn't interested in getting anyone into his life right now as he had a secret mission to fulfill that was an integral part of his dark past.

"Okay," he said with finality, "drink your coffee and blurt it out, will you? What happened to Jade? Where is she?"

Ann sipped the coffee pretending to enjoy the drink even as her mind raced for the appropriate answer. She couldn't tell him the truth. No. She couldn't do that to Jade. Especially if he is the one Jade had told her about. "Mr. McKay, these are questions you must ask the police, not me. They would know better. How would I know which Jade you are referring to?"

Phil was red with anger even as he got up and towered over her. He climbed the bed towards her and caught her head between his hands and made her look at him in the eye forcibly, "Look at me. Don't think I have been playing the fool these two years. Last year I was here and wanted to meet you desperately. But they had said you were unwell and couldn't meet anyone in connection to this. I tried several times over the phone. But you declined talking to me and refused to know any Jade Jones. Then the last few months I have been finding out everything about you. You can say extensive research. So, don't beat around the bush with me."

Ann had tears in her eyes as she took sharp breaths under his face over her. He didn't have a clue what was happening to her the way he was holding her. She was about to go into that panic attack again as this act of his was bringing violent flashbacks from the past to her mind. He seemed to soften up and loosened his grip over her. But he didn't let her go completely.

Ann pleaded tearfully breathing heavily, "Look I...I... feel you are a ...good man. Maybe life has hardened you.... but fear God and let me go. For heaven's sake .... please."

Phil now set her free with a jerk. Even as he moved away from the bed, he smirked sarcastically saying, "God...and who is God? That I should fear Him...do you fear Him? I feel you only fear men like me from what little I know of you. Not God. So, what fear of God do you talk to me about?"

Ann looked up at him surprised. Wasn't he right? If she feared God as she asked him to, why would she fear mere men? That made sense for the first time.

"So, you don't believe in God?" she asked, understanding he was an atheist.

Phil looked her in the eye from where he stood. "What happens by believing in Him? What have you found in doing so? It's not enough to even help you overcome your fears whatever they are. I lost all I have loved in my life. Every one of them...If God is there then I will surely believe Him if He helps me find her."

With that, he walked out of the room banging the door behind him leaving an emotional and perplexed Ann staring at the door.

Chapter 5

Phil had prepared quite a tasty dinner of spaghetti and cheese with broccoli. He had stocked up in advance as he knew what he was to do and how difficult this could get. She was a hard nut to crack as Nurse Lara had said in another context that morning. But he had just the solid hammer that could break the nut and quickly, he thought. He served the meal in a bowl and put two plates on the small round dining table and went off to call her to dinner. As he knocked and opened the door of the bedroom she was not there on the bed. He looked around the room and rushed towards the bathroom. It was shut.

He called out to her, "Hey Ms. Gomez, dinner is ready. Come and have it. It tastes good only when eaten hot."

There was no reply. He again called out her name. No reply again. He got suspicious and began banging the door of the bathroom. And finally, he broke the lock to find no one there. Then he noticed that one of the sliding windowpanes was open in the bathroom and the wind was blowing a little rain inside. She had run away. The insolent creature. But the woods were very thick where they were right now. She wouldn't be able to find a way out on her own at this hour. Nevertheless, he didn't want to take a chance. So, he ran out of the cottage main door little bothered about the downpour. He followed the path from the windowpane. She had left muddy footprints along.

Ann was running through the blotched-up path in the woods due to the rains. She had slipped twice and was fully wet and dirty all over. Her head was hurting badly, and she was crying, as she was again clueless as to which path to take to get out of there. Her car was still towed to his vehicle. The horrible swine. If he was the example of men out there, she was better off without them forever, she thought. There was just this one nerd in high school, Bill, who was such a sweet gentle boy to her. She knew he would never hurt her, and she had even started to make friends with him. Then he went ahead and asked her to prom. Of course, she declined and that was the last of their friendship. It was too much for her even with someone like Bill. And here was this absurd, male chauvinist pig of a man. How dare he kidnap her? Yes, she knew about Jade. In fact, all that had to be known. But she wouldn't tell him, ever. He could eat his heart out. But running without thinking wasn't getting Ann anywhere either as she came to an open patch between the labyrinth of pine trees and narrow paths.

It was a moonless night; so quite dark that her eyes had adjusted to it. But there was not a soul to ask for help. She was all alone in the dead of the night and fully drenched to her skin in the cold out there. She fell on her knees even as she shouted on top of her voice, "Oh, how I hate you, Phil McKay! Whoever you are.... I hate you...I hate all the men ever on this planet. Except my dad...and mom...and..," the last word was lost in her emotionally choked voice.

Phil stood paralyzed at a distance behind her as he heard her shout those words out. He suddenly felt very sorry for her. He slowly went up to her and picked her up to stand before him. She looked so frail and so vulnerable that moment and he gently moved her wet hair from her face. She kept looking at him as his eyes looked deep into hers. She shivered. He realized she needed to be warm as soon as possible or she might fall sick. But it was now going to be an uphill walk. She wouldn't be able to make it. So, without warning, he picked her up in his arms and began walking upwards. Ann wanted to protest but was too weak to do so. So, she let herself be limp in his arms as her head helplessly fell on his chest. She could hear his heart in a rhythmic beat like the tribal drums in a jungle she thought. She loved writing poetry. That was her hobby. Could she make one at this moment? *Absurd!* She chided herself.

"Enough trouble for a day I guess Ms. Gomez? You sure are a pain," he said indignantly, as he put her down in between the path after walking quite a bit without a break. He needed some breath, and she wasn't that light to carry. Surely her bones were heavy for she looked very slim. They were anyway very near now to the cottage.

Ann was angry with him and expressed it to him for the first time when he tried picking her up again. "Leave me alone. Thanks for carrying me so far. I can walk it up myself the rest of the way. And if you are forgetting let me remind you. It's because of you we are in this situation."

Phil was taken aback. He said with an amused sarcasm, "Oh my, me. Ms. Gomez gets angry too other than to sob like a cry baby all the time."

Ann began walking up muttering under her breath. "I will have you pay for this...wait and watch Phil McKay...."

She was surprised at herself and the emotions this man generated in her. To react with this level of anger in the presence of a stranger was something she didn't know she could do before this. It somehow made her feel stronger. Even as Ann walked without looking back not knowing where she was headed in her anger, she saw him overtake her in a few long strides and he caught her hand pulling her in the opposite direction to where she was headed.

"That's the wrong path...," he said without looking at her.

"Any path away from you would be right," Ann said, even as she freed her hand with a jerk and half-heartedly followed him up the trail.

Phil couldn't help but grin. Right now, she was like a naughty kid who had been told not to do something. They reached the cabin and Phil took out a fresh towel for her to have a warm shower.

"In the meantime, I will get changed and have the dinner warmed up again. Not that I am hungry anymore. Do you do this to all who get close to you?" he asked with a mean grin.

Ann looked at him with a question mark, "Do what?" she asked as she snatched the towel rudely from his hand.

He just took off his wet shirt and the vest inside as he continued sarcastically, "Make men lose their appetite?"

Ann understood the pun intended. She was furious. She was about to say something back to him when she saw him bare-chested. He had quite a fit body. Not that she hadn't seen a man like this, but only in the movies, never in person. She again felt very embarrassed by her thoughts. She ran quickly into the bathroom in the bedroom. Her heart was racing even as the flashback of her stepdad Kevin getting close to her for the first time came to her and she almost shouted aloud, "No, no please...I don't want those flashbacks coming back.... no..," she just shut her eyes tight as tears rolled out.

Phil was confused by the way she reacted to him undressing. It was strange that someone of her age could be so shy and nervous around a man in a country like America. *But then maybe it's her Indian genes,* he thought. He had heard from his friends who visited India that Indian women can be quite conservative when it comes to mixing with the opposite sex.

He had made the meal hot again in the microwave and laid it once more on the table. *What's keeping her so long in the shower?* He thought.

He moved towards the bathroom door and shouted her name, "Ann... Ann .... Ms. Gomez...,"

There was no answer. He was thinking, not again, as he pushed the now broken knob and opened the door. She was thankfully there, but in the hot bathtub full of soap bubbles, fast sleep. He took some cold water from the sink tap and sprinkled it on her face. She got up startled.

"Wake up sleeping beauty and come have your dinner. Then sleep as much as you want. 'Cause tomorrow will be a grueling day... or easy as you want it to be."

Ann just realized she was stark naked in the tub. Thankfully, there was enough soap bubbles to cover her modesty. But she felt exposed nevertheless before this insolent man.

"Get out, will you. No decency to just walk into a bathroom when a woman is in there," she said with indignation.

"I am least interested in eyeing a woman right now and that too of all creatures includes you..," he said plainly and walked out.

"Atrocious monster... who does he think he is...," Ann muttered to herself.

****

At the dinner table, both were silent for some time. Ann liked what he had cooked, and she wanted to compliment him but decided against getting warm towards him. Instead, she asked curtly, "So, what about that missing girlfriend of yours? Is she for real? Or just a made-up thing?" She then saw his engagement finger. There was a ring there alright, "Sorry your fiancée I guess...look, I can help you find her in our neighborhood, if you tell me about it..."

Phil cut her short, "No. You'll bloody hell tell me just the truth about Jade... that's all we need to talk about right now."

Ann wanted to divert the subject, "Oh, I got it. So, your fiancée missing was just a cover-up. She isn't missing, is she? And by any chance did you also send those goons to chase my car? Were they your men? And I suppose you were the one who hit me this morning too .... wait maybe you hit me this morning at the warehouse... Oh my God. You...criminal..," she said getting up dramatically. He realized she could be quite a drama queen when she wanted to be. But the woman was sharp in catching the facts, after all, she had done psychology. But obviously, he couldn't tell her that.

"Shut up and sit down. You watch too much Hollywood, I guess. Trying to change the topic will get you nowhere. Just tell me about Jade and where is she and you go your way and I go mine." He said pushing his half-eaten meal plate away and getting up. "Get the dishes cleaned up will ya. I am sleeping on the couch tonight. You sleep in the bedroom. I hope I won't have to follow you downhill one more time. Because this time I will tie you up." Saying the last words like a threat, he went outside the front door and shut it.

Ann screwed her face at him. As she picked up the plates she said to herself, "I am sure he hit me and also those chasing men were his men. I am surely going get you arrested Phil McKay once we get back." she said as she took the plates and forks to the sink and put them down with a loud thud. Thank God they were unbreakable plates. "Am I his maid? Get the dishes cleaned up will ya'," she imitated him.

As she began to wash them, she looked out of the kitchen window. The trees were swaying with the wind as the rain had stopped. She could hear the sound of the wind blowing through the pine trees making sweet music of their own. Ann was tempted to open the window. She loved to smell the fragrance of the pine trees after a rainy day. After finishing the dishes, she opened the window and looked out wondering what Phil must be doing outside on the porch. If she weren't so scared of being close to him, she would have gone out to the porch to feel the fresh air.

As she was allowing the wind to blow on her face through the open window, gulping down long breaths of air as if starved for oxygen, she realized she loved the hills and the mysteries they hold. She could forever be here and write sweet poetry on them. Just then she suddenly opened her eyes as she was startled by a strange sound outside near the witch alders and azalea bushes surrounding the cottage and then there was the expanse of the pine woods behind. It was a strange rumbling sound. Was it a wild animal? A coyote maybe?

It was very dark as it was a moonless night, and she could only see some dark shadows moving and make nothing of them. Then all of a sudden, a shadow stepped forward Out of the dark expanse behind. It was a human figure with a black robe and a hood covered on the head. The person was looking down so she couldn't see the face. But what she saw reminded her of the figure in her nightmares and this morning near the gas station. This was also exactly what was worn by those people who would come for the dark rituals in the secret cult her stepfather was a part of.

The hooded person outside the cottage had a black stick in the hand with which he wrote something on the wet mud. And then turned back without looking up and disappeared in the dark shadows again. Ann watched, holding her scream within her throat. She felt her voice had choked up from extreme fear. Suddenly a hand came on her shoulder and she turned with a loud scream. Before she could register it was Phil, she fell in his arms and fainted. Phil shook his head. This was too much for him to handle. He swore to finish his work with her tomorrow and get rid of this bundle of nerves quickly.

Chapter 6

It was morning and she was woken up by the sunlight falling on her face from the window where the curtains were drawn apart and the birds were chirping outside. She had this bad headache at the back of her head. She had almost forgotten about her injury last night when she ran like a mad woman. Maybe she had fainted because of the injury too. Then she suddenly remembered, "Oh shucks, I fainted once again. Oh no. One more chance for that obnoxious man to laugh at me... Ann... aargh... grow up girl. God, please help me overcome these stupid fears."

She looked at the sky outside the window and prayed with folded hands. She was again talking aloud to herself as usual. Then she touched the back of her head. She needed to change the bandage but didn't have any means to do so here. At least she had her medicines in her bag to ease the pain.

"Phil McKay, you monster, do you even care? Getting an injured woman up here and you don't even have the decency to...," she said it loud before she stopped abruptly because Phil was standing at the door of the bedroom with a cup of hot coffee listening to her blabbering to herself.

He looked at her shaking his head, gave the cup to her, and said, "If I didn't know better, I would have thought you keep fainting only so that you want me to serve you like a queen."

Ann surprisingly smiled, "Maybe you are right," she said with sarcasm.

Phil looked at her a bit amused. He went to the living room and came back with a first aid kit. He sat behind her on the bed and started removing her bandage to dress it again. She was surprised by his concern but didn't dare to resist him because she needed the bandage to be changed and couldn't do it herself. It was a very small wound but needed attention before it became a bigger issue. She was highly conscious of his every move as he did the dressing. Was he responsible for the attack? Now she suddenly had doubts about that. Oh, why couldn't she just be a normal person for once about judging a man? If he was who he said he was, then she needn't worry much because Jade had said great things about him apart from his over possessiveness with the women he loved. In that context, she needn't be bothered.

He asked her as he did the work, "What happened last night in the kitchen? The window was open, and it felt like you saw something out there? You were very scared before you fainted."

Ann went pale. She remembered it all now. The figure out there last night. Her brain had forcibly blocked the memory out when she woke up.

Phil finished putting the bandage as he said, "There it's done."

Suddenly, she left the coffee aside and rushed out without a word. Phil followed behind quickly. She ran outside near the bushes where she saw the hooded figure last night write something on the mud. She saw that something had definitely been written there but now it was all smudged up as if someone didn't want anyone else to read it. Phil stood close to her and asked, "What has happened Ms. Gomez, can you tell me?"

Ann turned to Phil vehemently and asked, "What were you doing outside the cottage last night?"

"First you tell me what you saw out there?"

"I saw...well...a black-robed and hooded person out here...just like.... well...I... I know you won't believe me, and I don't want to talk about it...," Saying this, she ran off inside the cottage and locked herself inside the bedroom.

Phil came knocking, "Ann, open the door...open up. Ms. Gomez...We need to talk...now."

"No, I won't. Get lost. It's all your fault for keeping me here," she sobbed.

Phil was losing his patience. Was she playing games with him? Now he had to focus and get her straight to the point. "Ok listen. Take my cell phone and call your friend at San Jacinto and your parents too."

After a little pause, the door opened. She came out sheepishly like a kid and was about to take the cell from him when he said holding on to his cell phone, "You will talk in front of me. Say you are with an old friend."

"They know all my friends. I don't make many."

"Say a new friend..."

"What if they will ask to speak with the new friend. Then?"

"I will talk...give it to me."

"But you are a man. I have never made friends with any unknown male in all these years except those in my parent's friend circle and our church community."

Phil looked at her unbelievably, "Are you a grownup woman of this century in modern America? What crap is this?" He just shoved the phone into her hands. And stood facing the window, with his hands on the wooden frame, looking out. "Stand near the window or you won't get good range," he said without looking at her.

She went and stood facing outside the window conscious that he was just at her side. She felt nervous. First, she called her parents who must be so worried she thought. After just two rings they picked up.

"Hello, Dada. It's me, Ann."

Mr. Gomez worriedly put on the speaker so both Elena and he could speak to her.

They both ended overlapping each other with,

"How are you dear?"

"Where on earth were you last night?"

"How is your head now?"

"Where are you right now?"

"Should we come back sooner?"

"Whose cell number is this?"

Ann calmed them down, pretending to be strong but Phil saw her eyes were moist as she said, "Oh ho, you guys can't you enjoy your vacation without having to worry about me. Please carry on, you two. Don't worry I am very fine. I... I am with this new friend I have made. His name is Phil McKay," she said looking at him and immediately looking away because he was again intently staring at her.

Elena quipped from the other end, "What? Unbelievable Darling! Is he a white American, Hispanic, Indian, Afro...what? Is he just a friend or finally you have...but then what about your phob-?"

Ann cut her off embarrassed, "What Mama...hold on. He is only a friend. Give me a break...and I am absolutely doing great...you don't worry about the phobia thing," she bit her lips as soon as she said it. She didn't want to mention that out loud. Why should any stranger know of her personal problem? Elena Gomez was about to say something more when Cristian Gomez jumped in, "Give it to me.... hey Ann girl, enjoy yourself. But do take care, dear. We are doing fine here. Don't worry about us. Bye, darling. Will speak to you later."

Her dad was quite sensible that way thought Ann. He realized that Phil must be just a casual friend Ann didn't want to fuss over and there was no need to worry about any panic attack if Ann is sounding ok about it.

When they hung up Ann felt suddenly very lonely. Phil kept staring at her and she got that uncomfortable feeling again. He said he wasn't interested in her so was there a chance of him trying to...No... he didn't seem that type.

Phil asked her suspiciously, "What phobia do you have? I am sure it's happiness phobia. Because all I see you is cry like a sissy baby all the time," he laughed to himself.

Ann remembered some of her school friends making fun of her phobia of men back then. She was very naive at that time and would quietly bear it all up. But now she felt like breaking a solid stone on Phil's head. She quickly brushed her violent thoughts aside, shocked at herself, and dialed another number, this time Britney's. But it went into voice message mode. So, she left a voicemail, "Hi Brit, Ann here. Sorry about yesterday. I left my cell phone home in a hurry. I suddenly had to come on an unplanned trekking trip with a friend. I will give you the details once I am back. Don't worry about me. I am safe ...and fine."

She sighed. Wondered if Brit would believe her as easily as her parents. Close friends tend to know you more deeply. Brit knew Ann wasn't the type to take off on an unplanned trek trip just like that. But what else would be close to the truth? She gave the cell back to Phil. He smiled and said, "You did well. Now I would like to get you off my back as soon as I can. Come let's talk. All you know about Jade."

He put his arm around her slender waist as he gently pushed her to come out of the cottage on the porch. She stiffened up at his touch. He could feel the tension because he moved his hands off her almost immediately. Ann on the other hand dwelled on it. What was this sensation she felt every time he touched her? This was kind of new.

Stupid you are Ann... focus on getting out of here quickly. She scolded herself.

They sat facing each other on two cane chairs on the front porch. Ann cleared her throat as she thought to herself, *If I ask his identity to confirm whether he is the person Jade mentioned...he will know that I know it all... How do I find out?*

"Ahmm...well this Jade ...whoever she maybe...is she in a relationship with you or what?"

"Don't...please don't play games, Ann. This one I can kill for...," he said the last words almost like a threat. He continued, "you very well know who I am and who Jade Jones is." he said looking stoically at her.

"Well ...I... need to know who you are exactly...I can't trust you otherwise." Ann was buying some time to think about what to do next.

"Okay. Bloody hell... I am Jade Jones' eldest brother Phillip Jones. Phil for short. She must have told you about me, I am sure," Phil said it out of exasperation.

Now she understood the name confusion. She knew Phillip Jones was Jade's brother. But he had used a different surname to mislead her. He was not McKay. And Jade had never shown her a picture of her brother as she had lost her old cell phone. So, Ann didn't know what he looked like.

"Anything else? Now tell me where my sister is. I have done my research well in these two years since she left home. And it all bought me back to Orange County and you. The first six months we kept waiting as a family for her return as she had left a note not to follow her. She can be very stubborn. And I did disapprove of her choice of some junkie friends. But when even after six months she didn't call us once...It was too much. For a couple of months, I relied on the cops to hunt her down. Then I got information of her last being seen in California's Anaheim area. I came down and met the cops there. They said she was last sent to a rehabilitation center near your locality. I came down there and got some information about a female counselor from a church social service team who had been working on her, you. I tried very hard to get to talk to you, but the concerned people refused, saying you are unwell and that you know nothing about any Jade Jones. I understood that you were purposely avoiding me, but it beat me as to why. That's when I planned to make sure myself and confront you."

Ann looked into his eyes and for the first time, she saw the pain she had felt for her mother in her past. His eyes were moist. He must love Jade a lot. Could she hide it any longer? But she had promised Jade by oath. And she cared for that girl.

"Yes. Now tell me... where is Jade? She was last living with you guys, I got to know some time back. She had been seen with you back then. In fact, through your social media site, I got both of your pictures together." He showed her a picture of her and Jade on his cell hugging each other. "Now out with your side," he said triumphantly.

It was obvious she couldn't hide the fact that she knew Jade anymore. She slowly began, "Yes, I and Jade became good friends less than two years back when she came to rehabilitation and she was referred to me for counseling through our church's social service wing...I can't tell you anything further because I promised Jade by oath not to tell you, of all people, anything about her. She was very particular. But I have an idea. My old personal diary at home....and there's no game in this, please believe me. You can take that and read her part in it. Everything about Jade and whatever happened between us is written there. At least if you do that, I will not be breaking my promise to her by telling you everything myself."

Phil looked intensely at her and asked, "Is she a... alive?"

"Of course, she is...," Ann replied almost immediately, "but let me warn you, you are not going to read very nice things in that diary."

Phil was relieved as he shook his head. Some head start. "I would like to meet her...please," he suddenly was this changed man, pleading instead of demanding. So much for the brotherly love.

"Please read the diary first. Then we will talk. She had told me you would come someday. That's why I was prepared to avoid you the last time. But this time you tricked me with a different surname."

Phil nodded his head assertively. "We will leave tomorrow first thing in the morning. I will try to fix your car today. But first I will check for some firewood. Breakfast is chicken sausages and pancakes."

Ann replied, "I am a vegan. I'll have the pancakes. Thanks."

Phil didn't answer. He was lost in his thoughts as he walked away towards the backyard of the cottage.

Ann sighed. The diary had most of her sensitive past also written in it. How could she just give it to him? No, she will have him to read-only Jade's part right there in her house and take it away from him after he does that. Well, at least she will be a free person again back home tomorrow. Wasn't she happy about it? Phil or Phillip Jones out of her hair forever. Somehow that thought made her feel strangely sad. Why? She had no clue.

"What's wrong with you girl? Have you lost it? Not him of all the men in the world after all these years and that too, he has kidnapped you," she mumbled to herself before moving inside.

****

Phil was cutting the logs outside the shed behind the cottage for the fireplace. Even as he stopped to take a breath, he heard a shuffling sound in the bushes near the pine trees behind. He became alert. He removed his small, licensed pocket pistol he kept handy in his roper cowboy boots and moved towards the bushes where he heard the sound. But there was no one in sight. He went back to the logs putting his gun away thinking it must have been some animal.

Suddenly a black-robed and hooded figure came out from behind the shadows of the pine trees and was watching him cut the woods and then the mysterious person looked at the cottage for a while. Then once again with a black stick in the hand, he made a strange drawing of some weird symbol like a spider's web on the mud, before disappearing behind the trees again.

Chapter 7

Ann was getting bored. She had the breakfast of pancakes. Boy, was she hungry with all the drama going on in her life? She felt like she was in some Hollywood or Bollywood thriller, she sighed. Then she thought of making the lunch today to pass her time, so she checked the pantry. There was pasta, olive oil, things to make the sauce, and also a bottle of black olives. Perfect. She got busy making some. If she had a TV set here or her cell phone she would be watching or hearing romantic Bollywood songs and do a jig or two while cooking. She somehow lived her romantic fantasies through these films as they didn't require her to be physically involved. Those were her stress buster moments.

After the cooking was done, she wondered what was keeping Phil out there so long. She didn't want to be alone there when the sun sets in. Not after last night. She decided to spend some time in prayer. After she had prayed for some time, she felt so much better and clear in her mind. It always did her good. She went to the dining hall area window where the outside shed could be seen.

There was no sign of Phil. Where was he? She took her new diary she had bought with her and sat down on the dining table to write a poetry on the first thought that came to her mind. Phil's heartbeat last night close to her ears, racing like a rhythmic drum in a jungle. She blushed. Maybe if she wrote these feelings down, they will no longer have any hold on her mind she thought. Poetry was also her escape. So, she began writing:

He carried me uphill and his rhythmic heartbeat sounded like the jungle tribal drums to my ears.
My head lay on his chest... the scent of him filled my mind and banished all my fears.
What do I make of this, something I feared all my life, could there be a chance to live that part?
O' God, for Your love's sake, help me to believe in being loved by the one who steals my heart...

As Ann reminisced what else she could write further, she fell asleep with her head on the table itself...Phil came in with the logs. He put them down quietly as he saw her asleep. Then he saw the diary. Curious that maybe she has written something about Jade or her whereabouts, he very gently took the diary from near her. As he read it his face darkened. He looked at her. What was she thinking and where was she headed? He didn't have time for this with her. He just closed the diary with a thump. Ann suddenly woke up with a start. She looked at him and the diary in his hand.

"What the heck...how dare you! It's so mean to read someone's personal diary. Give it here immediately or I will cancel my other diary deal with you," she said almost childishly as she jumped to get the diary off his hand as he purposely pulled it up. She climbed the couch near him since he was tall and jumped up to catch the diary when suddenly she slipped, and he caught hold of her on time to bring her down before him which left very little space between the two of them. His face was just an inch away from hers. He held her there with his hands and his eyes looking intently into hers. It looked like he could kiss her that moment. Ann's heart suddenly started palpitating and she was sweating on her palms. Her breathing became heavier.

"Aa...are you...going...to...," she looked at his lips and then looked away.

He suddenly let her go abruptly. "Well, you don't need to worry around me. I wouldn't kiss you if you were the last girl on earth. I am not into strange, regressive women," he said adding more rudeness to it than he wanted to.

These words hurt Ann more than anything ever in a long time. Just when she thought she had somehow begun to feel a bit normal after all these years of avoiding men like the plague. Serves her right. Does anyone get carried away with your kidnapper? Stupid. *Too much Hollywood and Bollywood, Ananya,* she thought to herself.

Phil lit the fire like an expert. She kept noticing him from the corner of her eyes as she sat cozily on the couch.

"He read my poetry. Did he know it was about him? Shucks. What a fool. I shouldn't have kept the diary open. Well at least I know that he is clearly not interested in me so cut the crap here," she spoke to herself under her breath as she often did.

Ann thought to herself, that she was so much better off and settled in her feelings until this 'ogre' Phil showed up and this whole kidnapping fiasco happened. She almost laughed at her connotation of him. Ogre! "Phil the Ogre," she said a bit loudly and chuckled.

He heard it and noticed her chuckle. She saw him looking at her and went red in her face as she thought to herself, *How silly Ann. Now it will definitely take time for things to become normal for you again. If you can call that normal. But at least for once, I did overcome a part of my phobia if not all by God's grace. At least like a normal person I am also capable of being attracted to a man even if he is an 'ogre',* she thought with a smile.

But anything beyond that was still a big question mark for her. Because the scars on her psyche were too deep. Yet it has to be faced someday. Who's to know, maybe now she will start feeling normal around other men too. Matt Johnson too, who was very keenly interested in her. She will just have to wait and watch.

That night after going to bed she was only tossing and turning as sleep seemed far away. Her thoughts were also going back to that hooded figure at the gas station and then outside the kitchen window the other night. Was she losing her mind? Did she imagine it all? After all, she had learned in psychology that childhood experiences can disturb the pattern of imagination in adulthood. That reminded her that the next visit to her mom at the mental health care center was scheduled for the coming week. She couldn't miss that. Sukanya hadn't recovered yet. But showed some improvement every time Ann would visit her, she was told by her therapist.

Ann could hear Phil watching something on his cell phone outside in the living room indicating he wasn't asleep either. She kept looking at the windows of the bedroom. Would she find that hooded figure outside if she peeped out right now? "No. It's all in my mind. My wild imagination nothing else. Back home I too will go see a shrink," she told herself seriously.

She decided to go out and make a cup of hot milk for herself. She was wearing a baggy night suit, the least provocative, so it was comfortable to go out before him. As she came into the hall room, she got a shock. He wasn't there. Just his cell phone video running by itself. She went close to see what was playing on the phone. There was some paranormal movie on it with again those black-robed and hooded people in the movie doing strange rituals. Ann's heart skipped a beat. What is happening with her? This was too much to be a coincidence. She looked around and all of a sudden heard some sounds up in the attic of the cottage. There was a light burning from under the door she could see. She shouted Phil's name but there was no response. She saw a baseball bat kept near the front door. She took it and began climbing the stairs to the attic. Even as she walked fearing each step she took, she looked at the door. Suddenly it began to rumble loudly from inside. Ann gulped hard, her head spinning with fear.

"The LORD is my light and my salvation; whom shall I fear? the LORD is the strength of my life; of whom shall I be afraid?" (Psalms 27:1).

She remembered aloud yet another of her favorite verses from the Bible. As if in response the rumbling stopped, and the light was gone just like that. As she mugged up the courage and held the bat up with one hand and was contemplating whether to open the door and check inside, when someone put a hand on her shoulder from behind as she gasped hard and fainted almost at once. Phil was exasperated as he held her quickly before she fell down. Boy, was he getting used to her reflexes?

"Fainting queen...," he sighed, as he picked her up, gave a mysterious look at the attic door, and moved down.

The next day morning on the way home Ann was silent and so was Phil as he drove his vehicle with her car still towed to it. It couldn't be repaired by him, Phil told her. Needed a good mechanic. The car was the least in her mind right now. She was so embarrassed for fainting in front of him again and again. This had never happened with her as often as in these two days, nor had she ever experienced those appearances or hallucinations whatever of that hooded figure before this except that her stepfather Kevin often came in her nightmares.

Phil on the other hand had lots on his mind too. Ann's strange behavior and her fainting every now and then and above all his missing sister Jade's whereabouts. Neither spoke of what happened the previous night at the attic. Finally, it was Phil who broke the silence.

"Ms. Gomez, I feel I have hurt you personally. I have no right to do so and didn't mean to pull you down. Actually, you are an attractive young woman. Just that I am not free to think of anyone right now."

Ann looked at his engagement ring finger. She had the look of 'oh I know that...'. Phil looked at her and understood what she was thinking. The truth was the engagement was a fake story as a cover-up. There wasn't even a fiancée anywhere, but he thought it was best left at what she thought it is. His entire focus was Jade right now and the mission that he was out to fulfill. He wasn't ready for a new relationship at this point. And not with Ann of all people.

Phil asked her surprisingly in a concerned tone, "But I just need to know something... do you have a problem around me? Or is it a common occurrence with you? I mean these panic attacks and fainting?"

Ann sat up at the mention of faint. Was it necessary to point it all out and embarrass her further? She wanted to slap him.

But instead with false politeness, she looked at him, "Yes Mr. Jones. I do have a problem with men. Especially with the ogre variety. I get hyper around them which can sometimes also be dangerous for their health," she said it as if she couldn't help it.

Phil turned his face towards the window of the driver seat so she couldn't see his amused grin at the unexpected humor in her anger.

She still noticed it and got wilder, "And Mr. Jones I must be very clear with you. I don't trust you with my diary. It's very important to me. So, I would let you just read the part about Jade right there in my house. You can't take it with you," Ann said quietly formally as he was being formal too.

Phil seriously nodded his head, "Suits me fine."

“Deal,” she said curtly and looked the other way.

When they reached her place, he got her car down from the towing equipment. Then he drove it to park in the garage while he parked in the driveway to the garage.

“What the heck. My car is working fine. But you said...,” she asked shocked.

Phil just stated without a smile, “Couldn’t trust you after your ‘adventure’ trip in the woods. What if you whisked off to San Jacinto or where ever else?”

“Unbelievable!” Ann proclaimed and she went in with him. In some time, she bought out the diary as Phil looked around.

“I have marked the pages from the time I first met Jade ‘till the end of it with page markers. See? Please read only these marked parts. Not the unmarked ones. You have no business reading about my personal life. So, I trust you won’t do that.”

Phil said plainly as he could, “Rest assured I have no interest in your personal life whatsoever,” he emphasized on ‘your’ more. But he knew he was lying. He wanted to know a couple of things about Ananya Gomez, if not all. What makes her into the nervous wreck that she becomes near men? She did speak of some phobia the other day on the call and what makes her faint at every silly instance. That part about her was a mystery to him.

“I will get you some coffee while you read it," Ann said coldly without emotion. Phil nodded. Suddenly the doorbell rang before he started to read the diary. Ann wondered who could be there at this hour. She peeped out of the window glass. It was officer Matt Johnson. *Oh no. He mustn’t see Phil here or one thing will lead to another*, she thought.

“Quick. Get into the room inside and don’t come out ‘till I tell you. You can read the diary inside. It’s Officer Matt Johnson.”

Phil was amused because he felt the guy had a thing for Ann. He went into the bedroom and shut the door. It was a feminine room with pastels and flowers and sweet nothings on the wall. And the room carried the distinct fragrance Ann had. Why has he affected anyway? He shook his head and focused on getting to read the diary. After all, this is what he was here for. Jade, his beloved sister, and the mission to avenge her.

Chapter 8

O outside in the living room, Ann had made Matt sit down on the couch. He was for once in his casuals, a white t-shirt with dark blue denim and a black leather jacket. He was looking quite handsome and fresh today. Ann sat opposite to him conscious about his admiring looks towards her.

"I just dropped in when I saw you were back home. Just to check if are you ok? You disappeared from the hospital and later you weren't home either. Your cell phone was not reachable. Is everything fine? Because there is another vehicle parked in front of your garage, that's how I thought you must be back. Any visitors here?"

Ann didn't know what to say, she just blurted out, "Well ya... yes, that's my friend Jones's vehicle. He wanted to park it here just for a day. And I had been on a trekking trip up in the hills near San Jacinto for two days. No worries, all fine."

Matt looked at Ann surprised. So, unlike her, going off on a trekking trip suddenly. "Wow, you went on a trekking trip? I would have loved to come with you. Let's plan it next time... together," Matt mugged up the courage to tell her.

Ann sank within herself. She was trying to be extra sweet to him so that he would go away faster. He was taking her smile and sweet talk in another angle altogether.

"Yeah sure. Well, Matt... I am a bit tired...err... Can we meet later?" She asked smiling politely.

Matt smiled. This Ann was more open and reciprocating than before. So, he tried his luck further, "Sure. Err...What about coming out...for dinner later tonight with me? I have my night off today."

Ann wanted to scream but had to handle this carefully. "Ok sure. Pick me up by 8 pm," Ann said, shocked at her response.

What the heck was she saying or doing? She couldn't believe herself. Hadn't she tried these things in the past? They turned out so embarrassing she swore she would never go on a date again. But come on, why not? She needed to be sure she was getting over her phobia anyway. At least she was making some progress here. Thanks to the Ogre Phil, she thought and smiled sadly to herself. Anyways there was no future with him, that was clear.

Matt looked like he got the whole world in that answer. "Wow great. Pick you at 8 pm then. And yes, how's your head injury? How did you manage to go trekking with it?"

Ann was taken aback at the valid question. What should she say? She said trying to sound as casual, "Err... well it's no big injury at all. Just a solid bump. That's all it was."

Phil was watching all this from the bedroom door in a way they couldn't see him. He didn't expect Ann to agree so easily for the dinner. That was unexpected knowing of her nervousness around even Matt Johnson that day. But who was he anyway to object and why? She was entitled to a good life ahead. And he was not the one to give it to her. Then why did it pinch him just a bit when she said yes? *It's complicated*, he thought.

As Matt left, Phil came out with the diary. Ann looked at him, scared of how he would react if he had read it all. He looked at her and gave a lazy smile.

"So, you haven't read a page of it I guess," Ann said surprised.

"Is it going to be that bad? I am feeling a bit apprehensive. But you have promised to make me meet her after I read it remember that."

"I don't remember making any such a promise to you. But I promise you now, I will show you where to meet her. Read it first," Ann said with maturity so opposite to her sobbing image last two days thought Phil.

"Can't we cut this silliness out and you just sit and tell me exactly what happened?" Phil said impatiently. He wasn't that great a reader anyway but also the fact was that as he began to read the diary his mind was more concerned about what Matt Johnson was up to in the living room with Ann.

Ann was quick to reply, "Then can I break my promise to make you meet Jade later? Well...I keep my promises to people who matter. I had assured her I will never tell you, ever, myself. And I am not going to. You are reading it in my diary. And that's what you will tell her too."

Phil suddenly felt a surge of admiration for the spirit of this woman who he initially found weak and sissy. She was quite a strong rock of integrity within and was fast forcing him to change some of his views about her.

"What are you thinking? Go ahead and read it," Ann reminded him.

"It's nearing 4 pm already. I think I will read it when you go for your dinner with your ardent admirer." He was afraid he gave up his emotion in his voice though he tried to look very happy about it. He continued quickly, "Also, I thought you had two weary days up in that cottage and then you even didn't turn me in before officer Matt for kidnapping you. Thanks... I want to give you a treat as a thank you down the corner coffee joint. I saw one on the way. How about that?"

Ann wondered what was on. Two handsome men asking her out in one single day. But she shouldn't be too eager to expect anything from both. For one she knew as her Biblical upbringing by devout parents, she wanted marriage to be the end of any relationship she managed to have. That's if she is ever able to have one. It was Phil who made her feel something special for the first time in her life. With Matt, she wasn't sure how it would go.

She blurted in shock, "What ... so, you will read my diary behind my back? And then read all my private stuff in it too?"

"As you said, I am to believe your word and so I did, and now you believe me when I say I will not. So? How about the coffee?" Phil asked curious to know more about her while having coffee.

Ann said matter of fact, "Sorry Phil. You are here today, gone tomorrow. I don't want Officer Harry or Matt or anyone else who knows me to see you and jump to conclusions. What I will do is I will make coffee for you and me, and we sit and have it in the back-yard garden. We have a little cute one there."

Phil understood and with an agreeing smile he said, "In that case let me make it for you. I think you liked my way of making the coffee," he said with confidence.

"Right...," Ann smiled despite herself. She was in a little happy zone after ages. Professionally there had been many but this was a personal happy zone. And though she knew it was temporary, she couldn't help but like this human part of Phil more than his ogre part. Yes, soon he will be gone forever but why not live the moment.

In the kitchen, she began showing him where the bottle of coffee was kept and the brown sugar that she liked with it. She went on her toes to get the brown sugar jar from the top shelf when he came forward to help her. He got the jar down. But she was very close to him as she turned towards him. He didn't move back neither did she come away from him to her surprise. She could smell his very musky fragrance as her head came near his chest. She dared not look into his eyes and looked down or he might see how she felt about him. But Phil made her forcibly look up as he lifted her chin. Even as their eyes met, he realized in despair the woman had gone head over heels for him. And she on her part realized, to her astonishment, she wasn't panicking, nor was she breathing heavily anymore, being so close to him. In fact, she felt this was where she was meant to be...forever.

He looked at her passionately as he moved the soft bangs of hair that fell on her face aside as he asked, "That poetry...was it genuinely from your heart? Ann Gomez, are you attracted to me? Come on tell me," he softly whispered near her ears creating sensations in her mind and body that she couldn't comprehend.

Even as she looked into his deep bluish-green eyes, she was confused, scared, and yearning to say a big yes all at the same time. But what if he was only asking to boost his male ego? So, she took control of herself and managed to say, "What difference does it make? You have a fiancée you are committed to and I have a big problem you don't know of and I can't tell you. So where does that leave us?"

He was so close to her face that if she moved a little their lips would touch. So, she was stuck. His past words resonated in her mind now. *'If you are the last girl on earth, I will still not kiss you.'* What game was this he was up to then?

Phil looked at her quivering lips. Today if he kissed this woman there was no turning back. He wouldn't let her go. And not just for the dinner with Matt. Even from his life. But she said she has a problem she wouldn't share with him. And then he was losing focus again of his mission. He was surprised she was having that kind of effect on him since she wasn't exactly his kind of woman at all. He moved away instantly taking the sugar jar with him.

"You go sit in your backyard garden. I will come with the coffee there," he said not looking at her.

Ann was disoriented. She couldn't think straight for a moment. "I ...ya ...yes... you make the coffee I will just sit...there... outside. Bye..." She felt so foolish.

****

That evening when Ann got ready to leave, she was wearing this gorgeous Chudidar Kurti, an Indian outfit that made her look like a royal princess. Matt had messaged later that it was a fine dining place they were going to. Even as she walked out of the door to Matt's car, Phil's heart broke as if he were losing something precious, but he couldn't understand why.

Once she left, Phil went back to reading the diary immediately with focus and intrigue as to what was in there. He started with the page marked for him. It was Ann's untidy handwriting, but he could understand it. Ann wrote,

19th April 2017

I met this pretty girl a few years younger than me, Jade Jones, from Nevada. She came to the rehabilitation center for a major drug addiction problem. Her so-called boyfriend got her to California saying they will live together and start a new life. He was a major junkie. And when she got to know she is pregnant and told him that, he just disappeared, leaving her high and dry...the wimp She later had an abortion.

Phil clinched his jaws he read further:

Jade is too much into the drug scene. And she has an association with some weird people she doesn't want to talk about at all. She almost seems

petrified of them. It's mysterious. Also, some of those bad elements are trying to push her into the flesh trade business, which she shared with me during counseling. After rehab, she needs a safe haven. I asked Mama and Dada if I could let her stay with us for some time and they agreed. I kind of find her so much like I was back then. Vulnerable and innocent. So, she will move here for a while 'till we can figure out what to do. I know it's very risky because she is closely involved with the drug peddlers and knows a lot about them too. And that's one of my reasons to get her out of here. We also get to know those sources so our team can help the cops to nab them. I know she got herself messed up a lot. So, I also want to share Christ's love with her. It changed my life which was so much messier than hers. So, I have hope for her too and I won't give up on her as the Gomez's didn't give up on me.

Phil paused. He was a strong man. The only woman who could bring tears to his eyes was Jade, his sister. And then there had been Maria, but that was when he was an adolescent. Today he felt his eyes moist at what Ann had written. She was something, this woman. He read further eagerly,

20th May 2017

I know I am skipping you much these days dear diary. But things have been very eventful lately giving me no time for myself and writing it all down. The good news is Jade is with me in the house as she has completed her rehabilitation this week. She keeps getting these threatening calls from those weird people and the drug lords. They had planned to whisk her and another girl Millie off to Mexico. That's why Jade had requested I keep her at a safe place for some time. There has been a spate of kidnapping cases in the vicinity recently. I asked her why she can't go back to her family in Nevada. She says she never told them where she is going and left a note to them not to follow her. Her elder brother Phillip is a very loving and but possessive brother she told me. She loves him too. But the raging hormones and weakness for drugs got the better of her.

Made her blind to all the love she had and has lost now. She wouldn't go back 'till she did something worthwhile with her life and make her family proud of her, she says.

29th June 2017

Sorry Diary. It's been a while again. Because there have been a few complications. A couple of them including Jade's case has got me into trouble with the wrong elements. They have been threatening me constantly. Saying they will get me picked up, blah, blah. I am not scared of them. You know my story. My fear is just one and that consumes my life, my phobia problem. Geno Phobia in technical terms. But right now, I am more worried about Jade and the other girl Millie. Wish they would find people like the Gomez's as I did to help them...

Phil stopped. Why in the world did Ann have Genophobia, an intense fear of men? That must be so disruptive for her. He was confused. Initially, she did panic when he got close to her. But from the way things ignited between them whenever they got close, he couldn't believe that she had this problem. So maybe this is her big problem she was talking about? He needed to know more about it. But first, he needed to focus on meeting Jade. So, he continued reading.

5th July 2017

Things got out of hand. I lost them. Yes, Jade and Millie both. My heart is broken today. Jade was picked up by them for sure, those weird people she was associated with and Millie felt threatened for her life and went back to them, I think. Now I am sure they will take them to Mexico. And then no one will ever find them. I wish I had Jade's brother Phillip's number, but she never gave it to me. Why God, why?

8th July 2017

I haven't been myself lately diary. With Jade and Millie's case getting messier. But there is good and bad news both. Millie and Jade have been found but in the custody of cops. They were found loaded with cocaine and other illegal drugs hidden in their undergarments and stuff. They were being smuggled along with some other girls. I know these girls didn't plan this. But the authorities will want proof. There is soon to be a trial. I hope I can stand as a witness for Jade and Millie.

15th August 2017

Have been very caught up lately. Jade and Millie have been sentenced to three years of imprisonment each at a correctional center for the illegal possession of drugs in large quantity. Glad I was able to bear witness and help lessen the sentences a bit, though I really wanted them to be set free. Millie's family was called in. Jade refused to call anyone from her family. Later I met Jade to counsel her. She cried quite a bit. She felt totally ruined. She took a promise by oath from me that I would never disclose all this to her brothers ever if they came looking for her. They would be broken totally, especially Phillip. I promised her I never would ever tell them.

Phil had to stop. This was too much. Jade was in prison? So, he would have to go and meet her there? His darling sister in prison. He shut the diary emotionally drained suddenly. He didn't have to read further. He kept the diary near Ann's bedside table and quickly went out. He started to dial Ann's number. He needed to know the location of the correctional prison where Jade was kept. Ann didn't pick up. He had heard her say they were going to a fine dining place in the Costa Mesa area. He decided to find her. He couldn't wait. But was it just for Jade? Or was it for Ann too? He was quite restless since she left for the dinner with Matt Johnson.

When he reached Costa Mesa, there was quite some fine dines there. He decided to check out the likely ones. Even as he decided this, he saw an ambulance standing near a particular restaurant. He had a gut feeling that it had to do with Ann. As he rushed there his fears came true. They had just put her into the van and were taking her to the hospital. Matt was standing worried at the side. Phil rushed to Matt.

"What happened? What did you do to her?"

Matt looked frightened and at a loss of words.

Chapter 9

Phil couldn't hold back his frustration. How come he had the ability to find and lose people so quickly? He shouldn't have let her go, he scolded himself as he sat at the hospital waiting area. She was taken to the emergency room.

Matt, who was horrified, had told officer Harry and Nurse Lara what had happened at the dinner. Phil heard it too, as he was there. Matt told them he started with ordering dinner. All was fine 'till the dance music started and he asked Ann to dance with him. After hesitating, she agreed. When they started dancing, she began to sweat profusely, her breathing became heavier and she felt a bit giddy she told him. She excused herself to the washroom and then the next thing she ran out screaming in panic, "He's out here, he's here! He's coming to get me...no... no... please..."

And she fainted right there with her pulse rate dropping low. Matt was feeling guilty for what had happened as Nurse Lara revealed a bit of her phobia problem to him and Officer Harry. After waiting a while Matt left as Nurse Lara assured him, they were there for her and there was hardly anything for him to do. He had to report duty the next day, so he better leave. While leaving Matt suddenly realized that Phil was there, and now that Matt had calmed down, he questioned him, "May I ask the reason for your presence here and also your extreme concern for Ms. Ann Gomez? Were you not here in Orange county to fetch your fiancée?" Matt asked suspiciously looking him over.

Phil was calm as he said, "Ann has become a good friend now. And I and my fiancée broke up the other day," he said confidently as he shrugged his shoulders.

Matt looked at him hard and left but turned back and pointing two fingers towards him and then towards his own eyes to say, 'my eyes are on you, watch out'.

Phil smiled and waved at him saying bye. As Phil sat there for some time Nurse Lara came over and told him, "Visiting hours are over. She's doing better now. Though still asleep due to the sedatives. The doc has said she will be discharged by tomorrow if all goes well...you go, home son...I will keep you informed."

"Can I go and see her just once? Then I will be gone."

Lara smiled curiously, "Knew it. There ain't no smoke where there ain't any fire...you sure care for that one. She is a prize catch I tell ya. A heart of gold. Just that she has been through so much. No other one could have survived. A strong girl that one is in there. Go see her, but don't disturb."

He went into the room and he thought she was looking like an angel sleeping soundly if there were any in reality. He had only encountered the demons 'till now. He went towards the bed and moved his hands over her head gently.

"Get well soon Ann. There's a lot I need to ask and tell you about."

Once in his car, Phil wondered what Nurse Lara meant when she said about Ann having gone through so much. Also, he had got a hint of her 'problem' in the part of the diary he read about Jade too. Yet so many more questions. No answers. He needed to know but for now, he had Jade to think of and the other part of his mission that was yet to be fulfilled. As he left the hospital area lost in these thoughts, he suddenly stopped his vehicle, "Of course," he remembered, "the diary and her parts must have the answers to the puzzling questions about her and also who is this mysterious person she is scared of so much." He was surprised at himself how every now and then his thoughts were turning towards Ann.

He turned his vehicle back to her house instead of going to the hotel where he had booked a room. He had kept her house key in the flowerpot where she had taken it from. He opened her door and rushed in. He went to her room and got the diary and sat to read it from the start.

Sorry, Ann. Here I have to break my promise not to read the parts of the story of your life. Maybe you can be helped if I understand it better what exactly happened to you, he thought to himself.

But as Phil began to read her story, he got more than he could have imagined. Ann's childhood was nothing like anyone's he had ever known. He was quite an influential man socially in Carson City, Nevada. He met many people regularly due to the fine dining restaurant he ran with his younger brother, Jeff, and the ranch he owned.

He would sometimes hear stories of people's hard experiences in life and he had a troubled childhood when his mother left them and went away with her paramour. Then a few years later his grieved and ailing father expired. He took over the responsibility of his younger brother and sister. It was a very hard life. But no matter what, nothing could prepare him for this, Ann's story.

By the time he reached the part of the forced drug addiction, the dark demonic ritualistic ceremonies she was forced to be a part of, and the sexual abuse of an eleven-year-old innocent girl, he was fuming with anger. He wanted to get hold of her stepfather Kevin O'Connor and make him pay for all that she had been put through. *The bastard*, he thought.

At this point, she had stopped writing her story further. As she wrote:

Dear Diary,

I cannot soil you with any more of the dark filth beyond this. Just know this, it's deeply dark. The secret cult my stepfather belonged to, they are the people who know where you are and what you do without having to meet you. They keep an eye on your moves. The dark 'god' they worship who is the devil himself, hates our souls. But the good news in all this is God loves us. I am convinced of that after the Gomez's came into my life. How else would I have been rescued and meet them? And that is why my story doesn't end here in the gloom. The church community and the words of the Bible have kept the sanity of my mind, despite what I have been through.

Though there is one thing I struggled with then and I am still struggling after all these years. The genophobia problem persists. I can't yet relate to the opposite sex in a normal way. The panic attacks persist. All I can say is it is becoming worse. The irony is I am a counselor for the youth in our social service wing and I am unable to help myself in this secret area of my life no one knows of. I have been asking God to help me with this. Not that I am worried that I may die a loner someday. I am okay with that. But my beloved adoptive parents who have been such a source of love and blessing for me, have been childless. Now they have only me. They sure are looking forward to enjoying their grandchildren around them. But I am not sure if that wish of theirs, I can ever fulfill. Will I ever find that one who will make me overcome my fears, ever? I keep reading these stories in books and watch them in movies. The forever after kinds. But the reality is different, for nothing here is forever.

Phil fell asleep on Ann's bed with the diary on his chest and was woken straight in the morning by some noises in the hall room. He got alert and getting his gun out he began to move towards the door to check. As he peeped from behind the door, he saw it was an elderly man and woman getting their luggage inside.

This must be Mr. and Mrs. Gomez. He thought. He put his gun away and came out before them. They were taken aback. Phil quickly introduced himself, "Hello. I am Phillip Jones. Phil...Ann's new friend."

Elena was the first to react to him. "What happened to my child...what did you do to her?" Elena Gomez was petrified.

Phil remained calm as he said, "Mrs. Gomez, I wasn't there with her when this happened. She was ...err...on a dinner date with Matt Johnson. And she is fine now. Most probably today she will be discharged."

It would have almost become a comic situation if it were not so serious. Elena and Cristian Gomez looked like two cute, confused kids, especially Elena, who looked like she was at her wit's end. A shocked Cristian spoke up, "Come again? Our Ann went for a dinner date with Matt Johnson?"

Phil nodded his head feeling stupid. "Yes...exactly."

"Well, we did get a call from Matt yesterday saying she has been hospitalized. But he didn't fill in these details..," Mr. Gomez said raising a brow.

"We spoke to Nurse Lara and she told us about her panic attack. But if she was on a date with Matt then what are you doing here in her absence in her bedroom?" Elena asked confused.

Phil was almost irritated. Her folks sure ask too many questions he thought. "Well, ma'am. I think we can talk this out on our way to the hospital and get her back home?" Phil asked in a very polite way.

"He's right, Elena. Let's go quickly."

Phil said, "I will drive you there." They nodded in agreement and left together.

Ann did a lot of rational thinking once she woke up lying there on the hospital bed. Her mind was racing with a million things. What is happening with her? It couldn't just be her imagination. Yes, she had an uneasy experience last night while dancing with Matt. It was a big mistake. She was taking things too fast to assert whether she had overcome her fears or not. But as expected with Matt it wasn't the way she had felt with Phil. With Phil there was something special, she couldn't pinpoint what, but she felt like it was meant to be. But then she was reminded it wasn't Matt who was responsible for her being in the hospital last night.

When she felt uneasy dancing with Matt, she excused herself to go to the restroom. When she got fresh and came out of the toilet, there was no one in the lady's restroom area. She washed her hands, her face, and when she looked up in the mirror, there in the dark corner of the restroom he stood, her stepfather, Kevin O'Connor. This time in a black formal suit, as if he were also there with them in the restaurant following her. He was staring at her with that wicked grin of his and then he said something to Ann which shocked her beyond imagination, "I have come back, baby. And I am gonna take you with me soon. You belong to us. You have been marked since your childhood." Saying this, he closed his eyes and crossed his hands at the chest as he babbled some abracadabra.

Ann lost all control of her mind and ran out of there screaming. The rest was history to everyone. Lying there putting two and two into four, Ann realized that everything started to happen to her after Phil surfaced in her life. Was it all connected? Whatever, she was better off without the Phil's and Matts in her life. So, she was going to give Phil Jade's contact and prison details and then say goodbye forever.

****

Phil reached the hospital with the super talkative parents of Ann. He thought to himself amused, *Ok, so this is where Ann's gift of the gab comes from...she has lived so many years in this atmosphere.*

At the hospital, they got to do the formalities. Elena and Ann had an emotional mother-daughter moment together in the room. Nurse Lara came in as Elena Gomez was hugging her daughter and sobbing.

Lara said loudly as she always did, "This is second time girl; you are comin' in fo' da same problem. I want you to believe you can be normal as anyone. Don't let this pull ya down evaa. Don't give up yet ma girl..." She spoke with emotion in an accent.

Elena smiled sadly at Lara's concern and shared in her optimism for Ann. "Yes, my sweetheart. I believe God has a good plan for you. No matter what the evil one did to you in the past. Your future is going to be only bright and brighter ...just believe," Elena said and kissed her forehead lovingly.

Ann smiled weakly as she started to pack the medicines and dress up into her normal clothes to leave for home. She would have to face Phil again one last time. Could she bear it? The very thought of him strangely bought mixed emotions in her. The longing to be with him was intense. The excitement that she felt with him made her feel almost like a normal woman. But again, the fact was he didn't want her because he was already committed to someone else, and she wasn't even his type he had said. Her mind was muddled about him, but she was clear about what had to be the next step.

After meeting her dad Cristian like two long lost friends, Ann quietly avoided eye contact with Phil. On the other hand, Phil wanted to be alone with Ann because he needed to talk. First to ask her about Jade's prison details. But after that, he wanted to also say sorry to her for so many things. He wanted to tell her that he really cared about her and that he didn't have any fiancée back home. It was a lie. And that he would make sure that no one would hurt her ever again. Especially her stepfather Kevin O'Connor.

"Ann, we need to talk urgently," Phil told her as they were getting into his vehicle.

She just calmly nodded and got into the car next to him without a word. The Gomez's sat behind. All through the drive, he kept looking at her. He wondered if he had been through what she did as a child would he have survived it? She was more than the brave woman he admired. Once they reached home, Phil asked her again, "Can we talk Ann. I know you need to rest. But it's important."

Cristian got a bit protective here, so he politely said, "Phil, she needs to rest, and I had a talk with the doctor. He feels she needs to be stress-free for the next few days. So...,"

Elena on other hand was reading in between the lines. She felt Phil was quite interested in Ann and even Ann was not nervous in that way around him. *Could this be the one Lord for my Ann?* She silently prayed.

Ann spoke up, "Dada it's ok. We need to do this. I will rest after that I promise."

Cristian nodded. She took a paper and pen from the bedroom. Then she gestured Phil to come with her. They went down to the garage. The sound of their talking wouldn't go up from there. *The right place for a secret talk*, she thought. Not that they had anything much to talk about other than Jade. Ann copied something on a piece of paper from her cell phone. Then she turned to Phil and gave him the note but stopped halfway surprised. Because Phil had a very different look on his face today as he looked at her. It was warm, gentle, and... what was that? Sympathetic?

"I'm sorry that I hurt you, said those rude things to you, was mean and even violent in my behavior towards you... please forgive me, dear Ann...I have been a selfish man... after what you have been through...,"

Ann understood at once and was furious. "You read my stuff in the diary, didn't you? You promised Phillip Jones...I trusted you...," she said with tears forming in her hazel eyes. She didn't want a man to care for her out of sympathy...Never.

"Sorry, Ann. I had to break that promise when you were taken to the hospital and I was told you kept shouting about someone wanting to harm you. I needed to know who and what had happened to you before I could help you and the diary was the only source that came to my mind so I..."

Ann cut him off. "Who do you think you are? God? Can solve everyone's problems? That's why your sister didn't turn to you for help. Because you always want to be in control of people's lives. Makes you feel powerful, does it?" She was being quite rude as she was hurt.

Phil was shocked at this unexpected outburst. He felt bad about reading her details now. He had no right to. "I am so sorry Ann... I shouldn't have."

"No, I am sorry. I shouldn't have allowed myself to be carried away in my feelings for someone who doesn't know their value. Why in the world did I think I can trust you of all people? After all, you have been hiding things and lying to me right from the start about your identity. Here, take this."

Saying this, she gave him the note in his hands. "This is Jade's correctional prison address, the contact number, and the concerned person to meet. All the best. So now you have what you wanted. Goodbye Mr. Jones. See you around." She turned to leave. The garage had a small door open at the side. *He could leave from there*, she thought as a lump was choked in her throat straight to her heart. She didn't want to fall weak in front of him by crying here.

As she moved, he came and blocked her path, "You too are quite selfish I think...," he said holding her close to him with both his hands around her waist.

Ann was taken aback at this sudden move of his. Ann swallowed hard, "And why do you say that? What have I done?"

"Helped me so far, will you not any further Ms. Gomez?" he asked with a passionate note in his voice he didn't hide this time. "Ms. Ananya Gomez. I have begun to care about you if you haven't noticed. A lot in fact. You have made me change all my previous views about you one by one. And yes, the truth is, I am not engaged to anyone. No fiancée is waiting back home or anywhere."

Ann wanted to say something, but he put his finger on her lips. This unintentional gesture of his sent her mind into a frenzy. So, he wasn't engaged. That made her feel so happy, but the next minute she said to herself, *Why should I trust him? This could all be sympathy and pity coming out for me after reading my diary.* She suddenly felt very conscious that he knew so much about her past. She felt emotionally naked before him. She put her eyes down with embarrassment.

His voice was heavy with passion as he said softly, "Ann, I want you. I have realized I need you. Please come with me tomorrow to Jade's..."

Ann couldn't discern if he cared about her. She looked at him trying to read his face and eyes which still unsettled her because there was yet some kind of mystery unsolved in them. Before she could say a yes or no, Phil bought his face closer to her. So that there was not as much as a space to breathe between them. He kept looking at her lips that were quivering again. She, on the other hand, was lost in the moment. All her resolves and resolutions of sending him away, being formal with him, all seemed in vain now. She wanted to know what the feeling is to be kissed by a man you care about. Then Phil said with intensity, "Ananya Gomez, I want to..." He sighed as he left his sentence incomplete, but Ann understood.

She wasn't naive. Phil was astonished at his own emotions. Till today he thought he had it all sorted out in his mind about women. But with Ann, it seemed like something else altogether. But he was still hiding his big secret that she was yet to know about. The day she would come to know, it could end everything she may have ever felt for him. Yet he couldn't help himself as he continued, "Come with me tomorrow Ann..." He sighed helplessly as he left off his grip of her much to her disappointment. But he kept his hand on the wall behind her so she still couldn't move away. There sure was the most magnetic chemistry between the two. But yet she mustered all the self-respect she had to say what she did further. "Go away from here Phil Jones...please... I can't...I... I don't want to go anywhere with you."

She was saying this, but her heart said something else. Yet it had to be done this way. He was simply feeling sorry for her after reading the diary. She didn't want his pity. Did she want his .... love?

Phil was jolted out of his sway with the tone she said those words with. He was a man who never really wooed women. And here he was out of his comfort zone for a woman he had begun to care for as much as he did for Jade, his sister. He clenched his jaws as he moved away in a somber mood now.

"Ok, if that's what you want, I will respect that too. I will be going tomorrow morning to see Jade and leave for Nevada afterwards. Henceforth you will not see me again. Sorry for all the trouble I caused you. Goodbye Ananya Gomez. It was great knowing you," he said it like a finale and moved out of there from the little garage door at the side without looking at her a second time.

Chapter 10

Phil reached the hotel he had checked into online and threw his bag with frustration. What was he thinking? He had sworn never to let his emotions get the better of him. He was so much in control before meeting this complicated soul. Maybe it was the diary that got him so soft within. But he couldn't deny that there was much more going on between them even before that, right from the cottage in the hills. But what the hell!? The day she came to know of his dark secret that now he knew involved her past too, it would have ended it anyway. Better that she refused him and helped him to focus on his only priority at the moment, Jade. Tomorrow he would meet Jade and figure how to get her out before her term by proving her innocence. He also had to think of a way to fulfill the second part of his mission. But before that, he needed to make some important calls and surf the internet on his laptop for some important information.

The whole day Ann felt like it was the end of the road for her. There was a deep sadness and gloom that even her parents could feel around her. She had lost him. The one and only man on earth she ever felt something special for in all her twenty-eight years!

"How stupid, how.... but no... I cannot imagine being with him all the while thinking he changed his mind just because he read my diary and felt sorry for me," she said to herself. So yet again her past had caught up with whatever ray of hope she had for her future.

Towards evening the house bell rang. Elena opened the front door. It was Matt Johnson. In his uniform this time. After Elena called him in, he said in an urgent tone, "Good evening Mrs. Gomez. How are you all? I am sorry I was caught up with duty calls and couldn't come earlier in the day. I need to talk to Ann very urgently. It's kind of official."

Elena was a bit taken aback. "Is everything alright Officer Matt? I hope it won't get Ann to the hospital again," Elena Gomez said with genuine concern.

Matt's face fell. He felt embarrassed suddenly. "About last night, I am so sorry Mrs. Gomez. I didn't know of Ann's problem. I wouldn't have...err...don't worry I wouldn't repeat the same mistake twice. Can you call her out...she is home right now?"

Elena liked Matt Johnson as he too was Hispanic, like them. And she always knew he kind of liked Ann. He would make a wonderful match for Ann in normal circumstances she thought. She said politely, "No. She just went out for a walk to get some fresh air. Said she needed it. She may be around the corner. You can catch up with her there."

Matt was relieved Ann was now good enough to take a walk, "Okay, thank you, Mrs. Gomez. Will see you soon. Do wish Mr. Gomez well for me, will you?"

Elena smiled and nodded.

Matt reached the end of the second road not sure which way she went. He didn't find her in the immediate neighborhood. He made a wild guess and went on the main road outside and there she was at the end of the most secluded road that led to through the woods, walking slowly. He was on his police bike. Even as he pulled over next to her feeling a bit awkward after the night at the dinner. Ann was startled to see him.

"Sorry, Ann didn't mean to startle you. But there is something important I need to ask you," he said with concern in his voice.

Ann looked at him without any emotion, but she could feel her body shiver at the thought that she was alone here in this secluded area with a man who desired her. "No problem Matt... sorry Officer...tell me."

Matt suddenly looked quite serious as he asked her, "Do you know Phil McKay is not the real name of the guy who saved you in the warehouse that day? His real name is Phillip Jones from Nevada, Carson City. He is a restaurateur. He lied about his identity. I want to know from you, is he still in touch with you, because he said you both are friends now? He was at the hospital last night. And...err...sorry I need to ask this also...did you know of his false identity thing? Because the vehicle I had seen in your driveway belongs to him."

Ann's heart was beating fast. If she revealed one thing, it would lead to the others.

"Ann please don't be silent. You may be in big trouble. Because strange things started to happen to you with his appearance on the scene if I am not wrong." Matt was insistent, and he was damn right too.

Should she tell him the whole truth? Yes. That's what she was taught by the Gomez's and their Biblical upbringing. Never lie. She could just skip the part about him reading her diary. Because that would mean she might have to give Matt her diary. Never.

"No. He's no more in touch with me. He left this morning saying goodbye forever. He was there all through the last four days with me. He needed to know about Jade Jones who happens to be his missing sister. Since I have been avoiding him in the past, he used a false identity to get to me. And...,"

Matt's face hardened a bit, as he said assertively, "What is going on, Ann? I am sorry Ms. Gomez. You will be called to the precinct tomorrow. Just a formal questioning and to record your statement. Nothing to worry about. This man Phillip might be behind your attack and maybe even some incidents in our neighborhood, who's to know?"

Ann nodded silently looking down. She highly doubted the last words but wasn't sure of anything anymore. After all that morning, she had heard a girl scream in the warehouse. But they had found no evidence there.

"See you tomorrow. I am on duty now. Bye," Matt said and rode off taking a U-turn from there.

Ann sighed hard. Could life get more complicated than this? "Dear Lord. Help me," she said a silent prayer.

As she walked trying to clear her mind with the fresh air, she realized it was getting too lonely where she was heading. She should have stuck to the vicinity of her house at this hour. She turned back to move towards the path that led to the gated community of homes where she lived. She suddenly heard something move in the nearby green thicket.

She felt her heart skip a beat. Not a soul around made it even scarier as she remembered the recent incidents of those unusual appearances she was having. She started to walk very fast, almost run. Even the footsteps of whatever was there in the dark woods nearby also could be heard running along. She could feel her heart palpitating with fear as she silently kept praying in her mind to reach safety. Why did her neighborhood seem so far off right now? The sound near the woods was closing in on her as if any moment whatever was there would suddenly pounce right in front of her on the road.

Suddenly, from the other side, she saw a vehicle coming towards her. She desperately moved towards it. As the SUV came closer, she realized it was none other than her 'hero' Phil. Was she relieved to see him? She just ran towards him as he got out of the vehicle and hugged him tightly for life. She was sobbing. Phil looked towards the woods. And then he spotted him ...there he was. The black robe hooded figure standing behind a big tree looking towards them. Phil clenched his jaws and protectively put his arms around Ann with a defiant expression that said, "Okay, I am here now. You dare lay a hand on her.".

The figure disappeared behind the trees. Ann turned her head towards the woods when she heard the sound again. But there was no one. "Something...someone...out ...there...it was following me...," she stammered.

Phil looked at her gently as he held her, "No Ann. It's nothing. Must have been a coyote or some other wild animal."

"No Phil. It was like the footsteps of a person. Not animal," Ann said with surety.

"Okay. Let's get you home now. We will figure it out. And tomorrow you are coming with me. That is it," he said with full authority. He had thought about it the whole day. From what he had got to know during the day researching on his laptop, going deeper into the mystery that shrouded Ann, he couldn't leave her alone anymore. He felt responsible for what was happening with her recently and now he was as much a part of this as she was. But he couldn't tell her his secret as yet, but gradually he would have to when she was ready.

He gently pushed her into his vehicle as she tried to say something. Once in the vehicle, she said as a matter of fact, "But...I...my parents will not allow me to...we are not a married couple Phil... and I do belong to a conservative community. They just won't let me go away like this with you."

"Yes, I saw that. Your parents are something else. And so are you, Ananya Gomez." His Ananya always came with an accent Ann noticed.

"But leave that to me. I know how I will convince them. It will be for a week or two max, after meeting Jade. Like a vacation. It will do you good to take the time off too."

What was he planning? she wondered. The thought of going with him excited her like never before. She had never felt like this. All she had known was the fears from her past that haunted her. But here she was with a man she hardly knew that well. And yet she felt like he was meant to be. There's just one more thing to clear and that she spoke up, "Phil. It's not just them, it's also me. I don...don't want you to sympathize over my past and feel pity for me. I don't need pity from a man at this point in my life...I have had that from everyone who has known me closely to date," she said, frankly.

Phil pulled over and stopped the vehicle. "Do you think it's pity I feel for you? That's the reason you pushed me off earlier? Well, I also was confused for a moment that it must be your past that I read about...then I kept thinking the whole day...' till I couldn't breathe at the thought that I will not see you again. Let's be honest and talk like grown-up adults. You know what you felt and so do I up there in the cottage. There's no denying the chemistry. And from what I can see, you seem to be like a fish in water when it comes to being with me. Am I wrong?" He said honestly.

Ann was surprised at his sudden and frank affirmation. How easily he explained what was so complicated for her. But he was right in what he said about them. The thought of him going away forever was as unbearable to her too. Her entire day had been doomed because of it.

"Okay...then you talk to my parents and see how it goes. I will not go against their will though," Ann looked down. She wasn't sure how her parents would take this. For them, marriage and commitment were sacred.

Phil muttered under his breath, "What have I got myself into?" he smiled as he moved the vehicle ahead.

The very type of woman he would have normally avoided like a plague, conservative, and that too from a different background and origin. But after what he got to know this afternoon investigating about Ann's past, his mission had taken a different turn and he needed to do what he was going to ensure Ann's safety too. The mission had to be fulfilled and fast. He was very clear and adamant.

When they reached her place, the Gomez couple were surprised to see Phil again in their house. They looked curiously at Ann because she hadn't told them anything except that he had gone for good this morning.

"Well ...ahmm...err...," Phil searched for words as he sat on the couch opposite to them. Shucks. Damn, it was easier said than done. Talking to her parents was more difficult than breathing underwater. Ann stood half-amused, half apprehensive, for the outcome of the conversation. The Gomez sat seriously waiting for him to speak.

"Well...I... what I want to say is that Ann and I are going to meet my younger sister Jade tomorrow and then we are planning to go on a trekking trip in the mountains for a week or maybe two. I ...err... ahm.... needed your permission for the same," he finished awkwardly and waited. It wasn't any trekking trip on the hills. His plan was different, but they needn't know now. If it were not important for Ann's life and his mission, he would have never been able to do this. Ask permission of parents to take a fully grown-up woman out. All the other women that had come into his life including his ex-wife Sarah, were women who made their own decisions.

The Gomez's kept looking at Phil for a moment. Cristian Gomez was the first to speak up with the tone of a father's authority, "Phil Jones. I appreciate that you seem to care about my dear daughter and also you helped her from what we know. Thank you so much. But we have some principles out here we follow. It might seem absurd to you, but we do follow the

Bible quite closely. You two aren't even engaged. How can I allow her unless it's a group of friends trekking together? To just go away with you without any commitment as such and we hardly know anything about you.... when we spoke to Ann the other day, she told us you were just a good friend, so we were happy for Ann. But now that we know how you both feel for each other well...It would be in the best interest that you two at least got engaged." Cristian felt he did well, he looked at Elena for assurance, who also nodded.

Phil was amused but controlled his grin. It would be too rude. Ann went red in her face and looked the other way. How could they jump to engagement straight away when she and Phil weren't even sure of where they were headed in the future? She didn't even know anything much about his background and how he exactly felt for her. Whether he even wanted to marry her or anyone in the future. She expected her parents to refuse to let her go and that would have been better than this. What must Phil think of her family?

"Well. Mr. Gomez, I wouldn't do anything to hurt Ann or your respect either. That I can assure you. But yes, I get your point and I have no problem with it. Eventually, this would happen anyway. So tomorrow I will get engaged to Ann before we leave in the evening," Phil said with confidence. Things were moving exactly in the direction he wanted them to.

Ann almost jumped out of her skin. Was she dreaming? Phil the 'Ogre' said he wouldn't kiss her if she were the last woman on earth and that he wasn't into women of her kind. He was going to officially commit to her? After five days of a turbulent time together?

Elena Gomez was the first to jump up with joy and said, "My son, what a great day this is. I cannot tell you how happy I am. Thank you for making my Ann happy after all these years." She went ahead and hugged him. She was short so he had to bend down. It felt warm and awkward at the same time for him to have a motherly figure hug him this way. He didn't remember last when his mother had hugged him. Even he, though a strong grownup man on the outside, needed that kind of warmth he realized.

Mr. Gomez was a bit more practical and couldn't help but add frankly, "Well that would be great. We look forward to that, son. But let me be clear. It's just an engagement, not a wedding. You need to remember the limits it implies."

Ann was now even more embarrassed as she looked at Phil apologetically. He assured her with a smile. "Not to worry sir. She will be well-taken care of and the...err. limits too. I have also a younger brother Jeff and his family in Carson City, Nevada. We together run a popular fine-dining joint near the Tahoe Lake area. And I have a ranch near my home next to a beautiful lake a little outside Carson City, along with a decent income too. But Ann needs to know something more important before she decides to get engaged with me... I was married once, three years back for a year before I got a divorce based on adultery. My wife Sarah cheated on me on various occasions. If after this she still wants to, then we will get engaged tomorrow." He looked at Ann hopefully. She needed to say this yes for her good.

Ann straightened up at this piece of information. Sarah. So, she had won his heart to the altar before this. Ann felt a pang of jealousy here. But it puzzled her how could someone have Phil Jones as a husband and then cheat on him? "Well, I have no qualms about that. As long as it wasn't you who cheated. But I do want you to be sure of your feelings about this and not regret it later. Because for me, this must lead to marriage Phil," she said affirmatively. Ann was very clear about her stand on such matters.

Phil smiled and said, "Well, in that case, let's get married by tomorrow itself?" He asked with a serious tone.

Ann was super shocked at what he just said. They had barely met five days back and he was asking to get married tomorrow? He was crazy or what? Cristian and Elena looked at him with their mouths open shocked.

"What's the hurry, son? A marriage needs lots of planning and proper arrangements. we will surely plan it out if both of you are ready but not before a month from now."

Elena added her bit not wanting to lose the moment, "In fact I was thinking of a Christmas wedding? It's hardly two and a half months from now? What say?"

Ann just held her hands up, "Wait. This is my wedding you guys are planning. Let me talk also. Phil, are you serious about the proposal for tomorrow? You can't be. Come on. This is no child's play. Whatever did you think to say that?" She watched him as he had this somber expression.

Phil suddenly changed his expression and started grinning naughtily as he said, "Got you guys, didn't I? Well, I was joking, come on. I know that's not possible in a day." *Unless* he thought to himself, *it happened in a place where it can be done in a day. Las Vegas.* He already had it planned. Because it was necessary the wedding happen immediately without delay as that was the criteria for Ann to be broken out of her inevitable destiny. He knew traditionally it would never happen on time.

Ann looked relieved that he said he was just joking. She wasn't mentally prepared for marriage yet and not tomorrow at any cost.

Cristian laughed loudly, "Well that was a solid one, son. You got us for a moment. So, the engagement plan is on." He shook hands with Phil and patted his back. Phil nodded.

Later while he had coffee with Ann sitting in their backyard garden, Ann told him all about Matt Johnson calling her to the precinct the next day to take her statement about Phil hiding his real identity.

"You will not go alone, Ann. I will come with you but after our engagement. I know what has to be said there. And then we will leave to meet Jade at the correctional center," Phil said with a confidence that helped ease Ann's fears as she asked him, "And after that, where are we going? Are we going trekking someplace nearby?"

Phil winked at her and said, "That's a secret. You will know soon. Trust me," Phil smiled knowingly, he was very close to fulfilling his mission for her and through her.

Chapter 11

The next day Phil was at Ann's home by 12 pm sharp. He had shaved but still had a slight stubble that suited him. He wore a formal off-white shirt with the first two buttons unbuttoned and black trousers and black formal shoes. He looked very handsome today. He had checked out of the hotel as they were to travel that evening itself. When he reached Ann's home, Elena welcomed him with a warm smile. He kind of took to her instantly.

Must be the lack of having a mother in his life all these years, he reasoned. He never saw his real mother ever again after she left. In his resentment he never tried finding out about her too nor did his father. He just kept waiting for her to return. But Phil's younger brother Jeff did miss her a lot. He was just six when she left and didn't understand back then what had happened. Phil was old enough to do so.

Ann felt quite nervous as she came out of her bedroom dressed in an Indian costume, a saree drape. It was chiffon in lemon yellow color and she wore a halter neck brocade blouse with it. The saree gave her waist a very slender look. She also looked quite tall and gorgeous in it with her wavy hair open and a pair of lovely long earrings to match the thin gold border of her saree. She always wanted to wear this one for a special occasion when she got it from a designer selling Indian clothes.

She had learned online how to wear a saree perfectly. Once she had worn a similar saree for a community function and Matt Johnson and several other men had complimented her so much that she stopped wearing it after that.

Phil didn't understand the costume as he had only seen something similar online sometime. But he understood well that it was an Indian costume that looked gorgeous on Ann making her look even more exotic than ever. And not to mention desirable as his eyes drifted to her slender waist on the open side of the saree.

Ann was conscious of his admiring look and she couldn't help but blush. Phil was surprised as he saw a couple of more people there in the house. There were a few of Ann's age group probably her colleagues he thought and a few couples. Cristian introduced them all to him as people from their church community, two of them being the pastor couple of the church. Phil had got a beautiful diamond ring on the way there. While Elena had chosen the ring for Ann to put on Phil. This was all happening in such a hurry, but no one complained. It was high time for Ann they all felt. Phil went close to Ann who was a bit tensed as she stood awkwardly praying in her heart, *God, I hope I am doing the right thing. Help me, I hardly know him other than that I love him...*

"Why so nervous, gorgeous woman? You are looking like a mermaid right now," Phil flirted with her touching her cheek lightly with his fingers. Her Indian costume did give her the mermaid kind of silhouette.

Ann blushed quite a bit as she looked down shyly. She had received many compliments in the past. But not from anyone who mattered to her. Phil was amused. Not in this century and this part of the earth would he ever find another one like Ann who moved at his every touch and blushed at his every move.

The engagement took place quickly, even as he put the ring into her finger looking at her intently. He knew what had to be

done after they met Jade. They would leave for Las Vegas. After what he got to know to research the strange happenings around Ann and where it was all going to lead for her eventually, he had no time to waste. Each moment was precious. That is why he came back so urgently last night to meet her despite saying goodbye earlier. Her dark past was fast closing in on her without her knowing it and only he knew that. And also, how to get her out of it.

Ann was sweating a bit and was having a little heavy breathing too, all the signs of her phobia as she held the ring in her hand. But the excitement of becoming Phil's fiancée was far stronger than that. It overcame her nervousness as she put the ring into his finger finally. And he kissed her on the lips. She looked down consciously. This was the beginning of a new chapter of her life. She couldn't believe it as she thanked God profusely from her heart. This was nothing less than a miracle for her.

As all congratulated them, the Gomez's had tears in their eyes, and they kissed them both. Phil was awkward but calm through it all. It would take him time to get used to so much mushiness.

Later on, Ann discussed with her colleagues about the work there and the Gomez's assured her it will be taken care of in her absence. She hadn't taken a vacation for almost two years now, actually not after the Jade and Millie case and she needed the time off. Ann felt as if they were all seeing her off to her honeymoon, not a short vacation. She blushed at what that would be like too someday.

Someday... She sighed. It would be so wonderful to walk up the aisle to be Phil's bride but for that, she needed to be physically and mentally ready to do so. She bought herself back to reality, *One day at a time Ann. Many bridges to cross before that one.*

Ann suddenly realized something she had forgotten and said, "Oh no. Phil, I can't leave today. Because I have a scheduled visit to my biological mother, Sue, at the mental health care facility tomorrow at 11 am. I almost forgot. But I also know you need to meet Jade desperately. So, I won't stop you. I can join you later tomorrow evening right there in the same town," she said.

That way she could avoid meeting Jade too whom she had promised not to tell her brother anything about her. But Phil was very adamant not to leave her alone as now he knew the dangers that were lurking out there for her.

"No. I think we will finish meeting your mother and then leave together from there itself. The town for Jade's correctional center is just two hours from here. We will be able to meet her too if we move on schedule."

Ann despaired. So, she would have to face Jade after all. Well so be it. Phil was making her face up to realities more than she ever would on her own. She had always been the 'avoider', never the 'confronter'. But right now, she had to also think of how she will present things before Matt Johnson.

That evening was a difficult one at the police precinct. For one they had to explain everything from A to Z right before Officer Harry and Matt Johnson. Phil took over and just avoided the sensitive issues that could create trouble. Like he presented the kidnapping as a trekking trip up in the hills when he saved her once more from the miscreants in the SUV and they became friends. They decided she needed to stay away from the city for some time. So, the impromptu trek and then he confronted her about his sister's whereabouts. The biggest task was Ann having to tell them about the sudden engagement. How to explain something so sudden to people who knew how nervous she was 'till sometime back?

Matt looked at her shocked, confused, and then disappointed. He looked like he could almost arrest Phil right away if he could. On the other hand, officer Harry Williams was happy for Ann and congratulated them both. He understood what was explained to him by Phil who also gave proof of his real ID and the honest reason to hide it, backed up by Ann. He also knew about Jade's case because Ann thought those cases were not in their jurisdiction. Matt on the other hand looked suspiciously at Phil as he asked Ann, "Can I talk with you, just five minutes?"

She looked at Phil as if to ask him if that was okay. Phil nodded sternly. He didn't like Matt either, especially knowing what he felt for Ann.

In the next room, which was Matt's office, Ann was a bit nervous as well as uncomfortable being alone with Matt. He looked at her ring finger with the stone sparkling and sighed, "Well, I won't ask you clichés like why him and why not me. I can understand. Each one has their preferences. But can I ask you why him? Why so quickly? It's been hardly five days, I guess. Besides, you aren't the types to fall for someone so easily if I know you, Ann. Please don't mind, I still don't trust your...err. fiancée... and am still on his case finding out more about him than meets the eye."

Ann would have retorted had she not felt the genuineness of his concern for her. "Thanks, Matt. You are a great guy. Just say that I am complicated. I sometimes don't understand myself. But this I do understand that Phil is the man I feel God has kept for me all these years. Well, I hope you too find your happiness soon," She tried sounding casual and polite.

"Sure. All the best Ann. Take care...and lots of it because you are gonna need it," he said the last words with a sinister tone to it that kind of disturbed Ann.

They were to leave the next day so that evening Phil took Ann out for dinner at a nearby resto-pub where there were music and a dance floor that half-opened by the beach. Thankfully, she had worn a light cream colored cowl neck middy and her hair tied up in a messy bun which was appropriate for the place. It felt strange now that he was her fiancée. She would have to get used to this new relationship that happened a little too soon. After ordering for dinner, Phil asked her to dance with him as a slow romantic number was on. Now, this was her next test. Dancing close to Phil without losing her nerves. Or she swore to herself, tomorrow she too would go see a shrink at her mother's mental health center.

He very smoothly took her to the open-air dance floor that overlooked the sea and was decorated with strings of led lights around there that gave the place a very surreal feel. As he put his arms around her waist, he felt her shiver. He knew why she would be so nervous and that she needed that extra time and patience to get out of that zone.

"Relax Ann, sweetheart. I won't hurt you or harm you. Just relax, okay."

His voice was enough for her to take a deep breath and let it out, feeling her body go with the flow. Even as she put her hands on his neck, she felt conscious and shy. He was guiding her gently on how to move. She loved dancing but before this, she had only done this kind of dance with her father Cristian during Christmas parties and it was a father-daughter thing. The other day it was hardly five minutes with Matt on the dance floor before she had rushed to the ladies' room. With Phil, there was a myriad of emotions erupting in her body and mind like a volcano. He slowly put his face near hers as he was mumbling the romantic lyrics of the song into her ears.

"You are the reason....", it was a Calcum Scot number playing then. Phil loved to listen to all kinds of music. Western classics were his favorite. Though he wasn't into mushy stuff with women, he was experienced enough on how to treat a woman to make her flow with him.

Ann had tears in her eyes. She was taking time to digest it all. She was afraid someone would pinch her, and she was wakeup from this dream. He suddenly bought his face in front of hers and said very passionately, "I think I can officially kiss you now Ms. Gomez...or maybe I need to call up Mr. Gomez and ask if this would be within the limits?" he asked the last words in good humor.

Ann blushed. She let herself relax as she was enjoying his flirting with her. She wanted him to kiss her. Now. But could she stand it if he did? Well, that was yet another bridge to cross. He lifted her chin, and she felt her heart miss a beat. He bought his face and lips down towards hers and stopped just close enough. Her heart was rapidly beating with anticipation. In this part of the world, a kiss was never fussed over. But with her history behind her, this was a big moment for her. Even as he was about to bring his lips on hers there was a loud sound of a woman screaming and shouting behind them on the adjoining road to the beach. They and the others rushed to the spot.

"My daughter, she was right behind me. Then I saw these two men with face masks on who just came out of nowhere pulled her and pushed her in a car. And they are gone....," she fell on a chair crying bitterly.

Ann got alert. Could it be the same gang that kidnapped Clara Smith? The cops of that area came there almost immediately. They took the lady and her husband's statement and questioned other people around too. Phil was very stoic throughout the incident showing very little emotion in all this. Ann found that to be quite strange.

That night back home, Ann was restless on the bed thinking about yet another young girl's disappearance. She knew the pain she went through being in the wrong hands in her childhood. She just got up and prayed for the girl to be found and united with her family. Phil was right above her bedroom in the guest room. He insisted on checking into the hotel again, but Elena wouldn't hear of it. After all, he was her dear to be son-in-law now.

Phil had given into their persistence because it was just a matter of a night. And that would also help him to keep an eye on Ann. But he was equally restless since the incident at the restaurant after which they left for home. The atmosphere of the place had changed and so had their mood. Phil had a sister whom he loved so much. He couldn't bear the thought of something bad happening to that kidnapped girl. He thought something and got up, got dressed, and quietly left through the small door in the garage down.

Ann had just got up from the bed to get a glass of warm milk as it always helped her to sleep in case of insomnia. Out of habit, she peeped out of the bedroom window. From the window, she saw Phil quietly moving out into the night as he walked stealthily towards the right to move out of the main gate of the neighborhood of houses. Ann was shocked. Where was he going at 3 am without informing anyone? She needed to find out. Matt's words of caution suddenly came back to her.

"Take care...you will need lots of it."

Could he have been right? Is there more to Phil than meets the eye? Her heart wouldn't accept that possibility. But still, she dressed up quickly putting on her jeans, her jacket, and also a coat as it was very chilly outside and took a torch if she may need one. As she moved out from the garage door so that she wouldn't wake up her parents she realized Phil had used the same door too as it was left open. She took the right just like he had taken and followed up to the main road. There wasn't a soul at this hour as the neighborhood of homes she lived in was a very quiet and peaceful one. Ann looked out left and right on the main road. No sign of him anywhere. Should she go left or right from here? Would it be safe? What if he had gone left and she took the right? Also, the thought of the footsteps following her in the woods the previous night sent a shiver up her back. She decided to go right as there were fewer trees and bushes on that side, a gas station was nearby too.

After going a little ahead with no sign of him she thought she will just confront him in the morning about this and decided to abort her search. Even as she turned around to go back, she heard someone call her name from behind her, "Ann...Ann...sweetie." She didn't turn around to see who it was because the voice was not Phil's, but it was a deep coarse voice that sounded so similar to...to...her stepfather Kevin O'Connor's! At this realization, she just took the momentum and ran towards the main gate of her neighborhood and didn't stop 'till she reached her house and finally took a breath of relief once she entered the garage door of her house and shut it tightly from inside. She was breathless and felt her blood pressure go low. She needed to drink some water with maybe a little sugar. After calming down a bit she turned to go up to the house, she was taken aback badly. There stood Phil, looking at her strangely. He moved towards her and held her tightly as she was shivering with fear.

"You are here...but I saw you there...out ...I...", She couldn't complete the sentence before Phil put his lips on hers tightly. She felt his warm lips stay on her cold ones because of the chill outside. He didn't kiss her fully. Just took her into a hug and stayed there for a while. She noticed he was dressed up and had his jacket on as she had seen him leave. "You did go out, didn't you? I wasn't imagining," Ann asked almost like a confrontation.

Phil looked at her helplessly. "You will get your answers very soon Ann. You just need to trust me..."

Ann didn't want to raise her voice and wake up the Gomezs. "That's funny. When you are blatantly hiding something from me. How can I trust you? I hardly know your past as you know mine. And I know you only since these five days and from what Jade told me about you. So how can you expect me to believe you, give me one good reason?"

Phil pulled her close to him and pushed her gently towards the wall behind her. The garage light was very dim. Yet she could see his greenish-blue eyes that still unsettled her if she looked into them too long. He looked at her with an intensity she hadn't seen in him before. "Because... I love you Ann Gomez...you nitwit...can't you see that? I love you more than I have ever loved before."

Ann melted at his confession. That wiped out any ounce of suspicion she ever had for him. She suddenly hugged him spontaneously. He let her be there for some time before he moved her back again as he bought his face close to hers and spoke right near her lips, "Now get some sleep will you. I will see you in the morning. We have a long day today," he said looking only at her lips all the time.

She wanted him to kiss her. She needed to know how that feels. Why wouldn't he? His breath smelt of fresh mint and butter. *How would that taste?* she wondered. She had heard her bestie Britney say so much about the French kiss. But forget that, Ann had never even experienced the peck on her lips that he just gave her. She went red as if he could read her thoughts. She just ran away from there to her room.

Phil sighed...women! One sentence never fails to do its work for the men, "I love you." It took all his self-control not to kiss her tonight. How he wanted to. But would it stop at that? He needed to be careful. She was very vulnerable right now. And he knew the cause of her fears. As of now, he needed to focus on protecting her and meeting Jade tomorrow. He knew he would have to tell Ann everything someday. For her he had come to California only to search for his sister Jade and that mission would end tomorrow. Whereas the entire truth was that his mission had only just begun. His mission to avenge Jade!

Chapter 12

The next day after saying bye to her parents they headed to meet Ann's real mother at the mental health care facility. At other times Elena Gomez would accompany her there. But today it was Phil. Ann felt conscious that he would see her mother's vulnerability and her strange behavior due to the schizophrenia. But Phil's smile when he met her mother Sue banished her fears. Within the next fifteen minutes, they were friends. Sujata was holding Phil's arms closely like a friend as they walked her around the garden area. She kept staring at him weirdly though. Ann noticed the glimpse of the beauty she was once. She had gone through so much as Ann did too. *With time all things fade here on earth, good and bad,* sighed Ann.

Just these three remain Faith, Hope, and Love. And the greatest of these is Love. (1 Corinthians 13:13)

She remembered her pastor quoting the Bible verse one Sunday service when they were having someone's wedding ceremony. She would have that for hers too.

But her mother Sujata never experienced that love ever. Ann had tears in her eyes that she didn't want anyone to see, least of all Phil. She excused herself to the bathroom. Once inside she cried her heart out for her mother's pain. And then she felt better. She realized she had been in there for a while and left her mother to Phil outside in the garden. She washed her face and then rushed back and was surprised to find her mother all alone sitting on the ground staring straight ahead. Ann could see she wasn't doing well today. She looked for Phil, but he wasn't there. How could he leave her mother like this and go? Thought Ann. Did he chicken out and leave? Maybe he thought that if the mother has such a problem may be the daughter could turn out worse later. Any which ways Ann had shown ample proof to him by her nervous behavior, hallucinations, and fainting at little instances.

Ann tried picking up her mother, but she wouldn't budge, and she was too heavy for Ann to carry. She looked around for help and much to her relief she saw Phil rushing there with the doctor and a staff member. To her horror, Ann saw that Phil's t-shirt was torn apart in the middle and his body was exposed to his belly.

"After you went to the washroom, she suddenly asked me if I was Kevin O'Connor. I said no. She said I was lying. That I was Kevin. And she started pelting stones at me. I tried stopping her when she.... well let's leave it at that," Phil said without an ounce of discomfort.

Ann felt super guilty. And to think she thought he left her and went away. How poor she was in her judgment of people at times. She felt sorry for having bought him there. "So sorry. I shouldn't have got you here. I am feeling so bad. I..."

"Please shut up, will you. I am no more a stranger. Your problems are mine too. But I feel your mother needs a change of place if you want her to improve."

Ann appreciated his concern for her mother. She also felt her mother needed a more homely environment to recover. She wanted to take her mother to India to her hometown as recommended also by the therapist. But going to a relatively new place alone with her mother who made her more emotional watching her this way was too much to ask of Ann.

Strangely Sue had never misbehaved as today. No, not to this extent at least. But maybe it's meeting a new person, a stranger so close that got her worked up and bought those ugly memories of Kevin back.

After fulfilling all the formalities and informing them she wouldn't be available for the next two weeks, Ann and Phil were on their way. Ann suddenly started getting second thoughts about the whole trip. Why was she going away with Phil without a second thought as to where he was to take her after meeting Jade? And that too after a hurry burry engagement? She couldn't recognize herself right now. How things had changed in just five days of her life. As if Phil read her thoughts, he caught her hands with his right one and said, "What is it, Ms. Gomez? Looking a bit lost? Hope you aren't regretting coming with me?" He grinned, looking ahead as he was driving.

Ann felt as if a live wire just touched her when he held her hands. She was more worried about her vulnerability around him than going alone with him. What if he got close to her and she got those panic attacks again? He would surely run away from her for good.

"Err...I....was .... just. No, all fine. Well, how long before we reach Jade's?" She tried changing the topic.

Phil understood that as he looked at her nervousness. She was also biting her lips today constantly, a new thing for her. But it did something to his mind as a man. How does he handle this bundle of nerves without hurting her? It was something he would have to do as the moments unfold. "Relax Ann, sweets, you look like you have been told today is your last day on earth," he chuckled.

Ann hated it when he chuckled at her like that. She retaliated. "You know I wasn't like this until you showed up in my life. I was well... quite sorted out. Very much in control of myself. And I am a counselor you know. That needs a lot of maturity and inner strength. So, don't write me off as some nervous wreck," she said it all in one breath.

Phil looked away grinning even more now.

"Look...look how you are making fun of me? Grin away Mr. Jones...at my expense. Ogre!" She said the last word under her breath.

At that he looked at her surprised, "Well there are women in Carson who would disagree with you. I think I deserve better than an 'Ogre'," he said, grinning.

Ann didn't say a word but looked away grinning herself. Phil silently pulled over at a food joint drive-in He stopped and looked at her. His eyes were blazingly more blue than green now. This happened when he was excited. He pulled her close to him. "That was better. The fiery Ms. Ann Gomez. I like it...I... also like...your lips..."

His voice was heavy with desire as he moved his lips on hers. Again, just a touch and go. He moved away immediately and got out of the vehicle. Ann just kept sitting there with her mouth open. Oh, why does he do this to her? Either kiss her fully or not at all. This was like putting burning coals on her lips and her mind too.

"Hey, are you going to sit there all day? Quickly come, let's grab a bite...come on...we need to reach Jade's facility on time." Phil smiled to himself as he knew the effect he was having on her. He opened the door and got her out.

Later that evening they reached Jade's correctional prison facility while Ann had fallen asleep in the car with the fatigue of all the days gone by and Phil made sure not to disturb her. *She needs to rest that pretty head of hers*, he thought. As for him, he was as nervous now, clenching his jaws now and then.

How will it be with Jade after two years? His little sister Jade, not so little now but she was almost eleven years younger than him. He tried to become her father and mother, but he guessed that was a mistake. Jeff didn't need him as much.

Maybe he should have been an understanding friend to Jade instead of an overbearing brother who questioned everything she would do. He liked his women independent, but when it came to his sister he was as conservative as Ann's parents, he thought.

They reached the facility and were told they would have to wait for the next day as visiting hours were over. Ann was relieved; one more day before facing Jade. Phil checked online and there were hotels around in the nearby township. And he booked two rooms side by side for both of them. Ann was so relieved. She couldn't bear to be in a single room with him even though he was now her fiancée. She was too vulnerable for that right now.

As they checked in and Ann entered her room, Phil moved inside with her and shut the door. Ann was terrified at this sudden move, "Wh... what happened? Th... this isn't your room .... I need to freshen up .... I need ...," she stammered badly.

Phil was amused at what she was implying he was there for. He gently pushed her towards the wall near the door, as he moved her hair locks from her face. She looked at those amazing lips of his. They were such a mystery to her. He noticed her looking at his mouth as he bought his lips close to hers and stopped. Then all of a sudden, he turned his face to the other side and sighed hard.

"Ms. Gomez if you were one of those women I have met in my life before I wouldn't be just standing and looking at you...but you are...you. And I wouldn't do anything to hurt you. I need you to be comfortable around me. But very soon I am going to make sure you will be. Goodnight." He gave a peck on her cheeks and went out of the room.

Ann's breath that was stuck in her throat just came out in a sigh. What was happening here? She was confused. She wanted him to kiss her, but maybe she was giving him the wrong signals with her nervous body language. She needed to relax in his presence. After all, he was engaged to her and she loved this man who changed everything she ever felt like a woman. One thing was confirmed for her after this, that Phil was a gentleman she could trust with her life.

Phil lay in his bed reminiscing of his time with Ann all these five eventful days. And also, he was aware of the dark cloud that loomed over her head. After meeting Jade, he needed to move fast towards his plan. Or else everything could turn upside down and he would surely lose Ann forever. As he lay falling asleep slowly, as he was tired, more mentally than physically, he suddenly was woken up with a strange sound out his door as he was a light sleeper.

He immediately dialed Ann's room number to make sure she was fine, but there was no response after many rings. He became alert as he got up and took his gun out from his jean's pocket. He moved towards his room door as he opened it slowly a little, enough to peep out. He didn't see anyone. He went out slowly and there he saw her down the long corridor walking as if in her sleep. Ann just had her sleeveless nightie on as she walked towards the staircase of the fire exit. He ran towards her putting the gun in the pocket of his satin pajamas. He slept bare-chested and that's how he came out, without giving much thought. There were heaters on in the hotel, so it was quite warm in there. As he closed in on her, he realized she was sleepwalking, looking straight ahead. She wasn't conscious of her movements and she looked as if an external force was in control of her.

"It's all happening too quick. They must be aware of everything. I too will need to move fast." He thought to himself. He couldn't jolt her out suddenly. That could cause more harm to her. He gently came ahead of her and stopped her as he turned towards her. She stared at him with wide-open eyes as if a wall were before her. He quietly picked her up as he moved swiftly to her room. She didn't resist. As he lay her on her bed, he got some water from the jar and sprinkled it on her face. She took a deep breath and came out of that state.

"Wh... wh... what... how did you get inside? Phil.... what happened?" She was trying to recollect something.

"It's ok...it's ok sweetheart. All is well. Don't worry about it. You were sleepwalking when I saw you down the corridor. Relax. I am here now." Phil assured her.

She looked at him with disbelief. "What!? Sleepwalking...me? I have never in my entire life." She almost shouted.

"Shhh...relax.... you will be fine..." He calmed her down as he sat next to her on the bed and took her head on his bare chest. But she immediately reacted lifting her head up. He once again gently pushed her head back. She was so awkward there, her head on his bare skin.

"I ...I will be fine now.... you go to your room...I'll call you if anything..."

"Shh...you talk too much Ms. Gomez. Just sleep, will ya? I am not gonna force myself on you if that's what you are scared of. By now you should know me." He said with a little indignation.

She knew him yes and trusted him already. But it's her head she didn't trust. She was now also sleepwalking for heaven's sake. But as he said sleep, so she obeyed without argument and snuggled up near his neck and slept. Boy, did this feel good. "That's why Eve was created for Adam and vice versa," she smiled to herself as she remembered the age-old story from the Bible. It did feel at home. With these thoughts, she fell fast asleep.

Next morning when she woke up. She was alone on the bed. Phil was gone. She felt happy that he was there for her last night. Though her mind started questioning her, *How come he knows it whenever I am in trouble? Every time he's there to save me on time. He seems to be quite confident about what I am going through as if he knows something that I don't? Is there truly more to Phil than meets the eye as Matt Johnson had put it?* Last night outside her house where did he go and then suddenly appeared before she reached back? So many questions. The answers only God knew and Phil himself. He told her he would tell her everything at the right time. What was that right time? Well, she would just have to wait and watch. And trust him in the meantime she sighed.

Phil had got ready in his room after asking for the master key as his room had locked in last night. He was excited about meeting Jade today. He got a call from Ann on the intercom.

"Hey, when did you go? You should have woken me too. I am getting ready. Meet you down in fifteen minutes. We are checking out right?" she asked.

"Yes, sweetheart. Hope you had a good sleep. See you in a bit." He hung up quite impressed that she said fifteen minutes. He had never met a woman who got ready in that much time. But it was well past thirty minutes when Ann came down from her room wearing a short Indian cotton Kurti in light green shade and a pair of blue jeans, her hair tied in a ponytail. She looked as fresh as ever with almost no makeup except nude lipstick and kohl in her eyes. For one he liked his woman with almost no makeup. And Ann was as pretty without it. He kissed her on her forehead as they moved out towards the parking area. Even that little gesture of his made Ann's stomach twirl. As they sat in the SUV, Ann did something she never could have imagined. She came closer to Phil and as he looked at her she put her lips on his for full ten seconds, before shyly moving away.

He didn't say a word, just smiled and started the vehicle and moved to glance at her as she looked the other way not able to look back at him immediately. On the way she called her parents and told them they were fine and meeting Phil's sister

Jade today. Then she called Britney who hadn't spoken to her since. She was angry with her for ditching her that day and going away on a trekking trip without any explanation. Ann convinced her she was very sorry and would meet her soon and explain everything in detail.

As Phil moved into the prison facility parking area, Ann's heart began to sink. Will Jade believe her explanation about how Phil came to know? Or would she hate her? After some formalities, they were taken to the visiting room. Ann hesitated outside but Phil just held her hands tightly and took her in.

Jade was there already sitting with her head down. Phil stood for a second looking at her as he left Ann's hand. He was in another zone now, the brotherly instincts taking over. Jade looked up. Her face had changed from what Ann last saw her there months back. She looked even more frail and sad. Phil couldn't believe it was his beautiful sister Jade before him. He twitched his jaws in anger. "Can you give us five minutes? I will call you back." He said to Ann without looking at her.

She nodded and went out giving a glance to Jade who kept looking at Phil with a stoic expression. Phil moved towards the wall of the room. He needed to get hold of his emotions before he spoke. His eyes were filled to the brim. He wiped them roughly and took a deep breath and came and sat down before her.

"Jade," he said with difficulty in a shaky voice. He touched her hand softly. That was it. It broke a dam of emotions from Jade who was silent 'till then.

"Why bro... why...why did you come here...I didn't want you to see me like this ...not ever... I ...I," her voice trailed off in her sobs.

Phil got up and held her head close to him as she let out her pent-up emotions. He was also crying in his way.

"Stop Jade...don't cry, darling. I am going to see how I can get you out of here before time because I know you are innocent of the crime. It's a set-up. And it's because of me they did this to you... but I will get you out even it takes everything. For that, you got to tell me the truth. All of it. I already know who did this to you. I am going to deal with that soon. But you need to tell me all in detail."

"Do you forgive me then, Phil?" she asked almost like a child.

"When was I ever angry with you, sweetheart? Disappointed…Yes...Not angry. I just kept waiting for you 'till I couldn't wait any longer." Phil said as he sat down on his chair more composed now.

"So, you got everything out of Ann, right?" Jade said assuming Ann gave her up.

"No. She wouldn't tell a single word. Had to kidnap her to get things out." Phil said grinning.

"What? Unbelievable. You kidnapped my dear friend Ann... poor thing, her." Jade was shocked.

"Well, even then she didn't tell me everything. I had to get it all through her personal diary." He said saving Ann the effort to explain herself.

"That's Ann for you. A strong woman if I have seen one. She is so honest it's painful." She laughed. Jade's face had changed color. Now she looked so much brighter than when they had walked in.

Phil smiled. There were many more things painful about Ann. *For one her conservative upbringing*, he thought. "Now I want all the details of those bastards who got you here. Quick. We have limited time." He said with his blazing eyes changing color in his anger.

Jade swallowed hard as she prepared to tell him all, "Bro... they are terrible. They will kill me if they know I told you everything ..."

"Jade trust me. I already know a lot more than you know. Just need some confirmations before I take my steps. And this also involves Ann. Her life is in danger. You will help both her and you. But right now, we can't reveal anything to Ann as yet." Phil warned his sister.

Outside Ann was feeling fidgety. Why did he bring along if he had to keep her out? She felt like she wasn't a part of his personal life whereas he had become such a great part of hers. From her diary to her parents, to her real mother Sue's condition, he had met them all and seen it all. Suddenly after what seems ages the door opened. They had very little visiting time left. He called Ann in, as his emotions were now controlled. He didn't want Ann to see his most vulnerable moment then. Not yet. She needed to feel safe with him first. Ann entered the room looking a bit guiltily towards Jade who put all her doubts to rest as she got up and hugged Ann with genuine love.

"Thanks, friend, for not letting your word down on me. So much so you got kidnapped for my sake," she said with a smile.

Ann smiled. So, Phil had taken care of that part. She was relaxed now. "How are you doing, girl? Sorry I couldn't do much for you. I know it's not your fault you are here. But you didn't reveal all to the lawyer who had asked you that time. I don't know what stopped you back then or who. Your term could have been much lesser or even nil if you had opened up and cooperated with the police."

Jade's face suddenly turned dark. Ann felt she looked as scared as at the time of the trial when certain things about the people involved were asked of her. Just then the officer came in and told them their time was up.

"I will be back, girl, and soon. Just count the days. Love you, my dear Jade." Phil said as he kissed her cheek, and they left the room abruptly. He just went to the window outside the room with the blinds and stood there for a moment. Ann could see he was emotional and was trying hard to control. *He surely loves her so much*, she thought.

During the drive towards Nevada, Phil was mostly silent. It was Ann who spoke up. "I don't want to be presumptuous, but I feel we need to go deeper in Jade's case. There is something she is hiding because she is very afraid of someone. Maybe that thing is the key to her freedom?"

Phil's jaws twitched as he said, "You are so right Ms. Gomez. You are being presumptuous. Don't go that way. Leave that to me."

Ann could sense his bad mood and thought it best to be silent. She fell asleep again in the monotony of the drive. After a while she suddenly opened her eyes she was alone in the vehicle. Phil wasn't there. And the area outside was very secluded and dark. Not a soul around.

She felt a pang of fear, "Phil... Ph... Phil..." she cried out loud. Where was he? She opened the door and jumped out. She needed to straighten her back too. As she looked all around there was no one. There were no streetlights anywhere. It wasn't even the main road anymore. They were in some vague place, cut off from all civilization. It was a plain desert landscape. So where had he gone leaving her alone here for heaven's sake? Then she heard the voice, the same coarse one belonging to Kevin O'Connor. She couldn't miss that voice anywhere.

"Ann... darling.... why do you run away from me? You can't. This is your destiny. You are interwoven in it forever...come, baby...come to daddy."

She felt her head spinning as the voice behind her came closer until she felt his breath on her neck and that's when she screamed loudly.

Chapter 13

Phil pulled over to the side. Ann was having a nightmare again. She was screaming loudly, "Please stay away! I don't want to have anything to do with you! Go away...go away...leave me alone. Jesusss... help me." She kept shouting without opening her eyes.

Phil just took her into his arms, and she kept pushing him away as he calmed her saying, "Shhh...Ann .... sweetheart... it's ok...it's just a nightmare...it's nothing...just a bad dream.... calm down."

She opened her eyes slowly and realized it was a nightmare, thankfully. Ann just held him tightly. She was shaking badly. Phil swore under his breath. They were moving things fast against Ann because of his presence in her life now and they probably knew of the engagement too. He had to take the next step as soon as possible. Get married to Ann.

"Oh, Phil ...it was my stepfather again in my nightmare. I ....do...don't know why they are recurring so often now. And also, I keep seeing him almost anywhere. Am I losing my mind? Tell me, Phil, am I going to my mother's..."

Phil felt angry and had an impulse to just go now and confront those responsible for her state. This is what they must have done to her mother too. Made her lose her mind. But he had to be very calculative. They were very powerful and so was their leader. And it was not in physical terms. The power was diabolical like nothing he had ever seen before. But he knew their secret in the case of Ann and he was going to use it.

"No Ann, you are not losing it. You will know it in time. Just have patience." Phil assured her.

"So, you do know why this is happening? Is it connected to you? Are you in any way responsible for this?" Ann straightened up and asked him surprised at what he just said.

"Ann, I am your fiancée. Give me some credit, will you? Yes, there are things you don't know about me right now. But have patience. You will very soon. Trust me, darling." He held her hands and reassured her.

Ann looked doubtful of everything now. Could she trust him? Where was he headed with her? How foolish. She had left the safety of her home, her parents, and community to move out with a man who was still relatively a stranger to her. Just a ring couldn't change that, could it? She kept quiet the rest of the way. Phil also preferred to be silent. At least she won't ask too many questions. After a few hours, they broke the journey to Las Vegas. Ann wondered why. Was this his surprise?

"This is a part of my surprise for you but not the whole of it. Tomorrow you will see," he said. He had already made arrangements for it. Just one night to go.

Ann normally loved surprises but with Phil, she wasn't so sure now. *Relax Ann. Just enjoy his company, will you? Wasn't this what you longed for? It's Matt Johnson who put these doubts in your mind. Trust Phil. He has not let you down 'till now. What have you to lose?* Ann told herself.

That night they checked into a hotel, this time a suite room where Phil assured her, he would sleep on the living room couch and she in the bedroom. So, she was okay. He on the other hand was apprehensive about the things happening to her. Better that she be in his presence in the night. They did some shopping over there before coming to the hotel where he bought her a lovely evening dress in emerald green and a pretty necklace to go with it. She looked beautiful wearing them. Then he took her to the popular casinos around and they had dinner at a popular restaurant there. Ann hadn't had so much fun in ages she felt. Especially because this special something was igniting between her and Phil every now and then. Every accidental touch, every brush of shoulders, every meeting of the eyes felt like her stomach had butterflies inside and made her realize feelings that she never thought she was capable of having.

She could feel the passion like a live wire between them. But at the end of it all that night she was afraid of staying with him in the same suite. Cristian Gomez's words, "It's not a wedding. Remember the limits it implies." came back to her with all the Biblical teachings she ever had to date. But Phil too was making sure they spend very little time alone as he purposely spent more time out there in Vegas with her than going back to the hotel room. He thought the more he delayed, they would be very tired and go back and fall asleep immediately. He didn't want to do anything out of his planned zone right now. Because there were rules in the diabolical world of the ones who wanted to harm her, and it could result in the plan backfiring.

A little later when they were very tired, it was Ann who said she wanted to go to the room as she was very sleepy. They had hardly played at the casinos as neither Phil nor she were into gambling. It was more of reveling around in the open streets. Ann had never visited the sin city before and was quite amused why they called it that, "I believe sin is everywhere. So? I think people in California are as many sinners as here or anywhere else on earth. All need salvation and forgiveness before they leave the earth to be saved from Hell." she said munching on cinnamon sticks. She loved them. She was speaking from her experience with spirituality.

"Oh yeah? So, you mean to say God...whoever you say He is, forgives sins just like that? Even such mean evil people like your stepfather Kevin? Or all those who murder, rape, and steal? How? Beats me." He said it all with loads of sarcasm. He was not into her kind of blind faith.

"He does Phil. That's the truth. God sent His Son Jesus to Earth, who gave His life for the forgiveness of our sins, on the cross 2000 years back taking our place." She said with more surety than anything else on Earth.

"A woman leaves her three young kids with an ailing husband. To fulfill her desires with another man and never turns to look back even after years. Your God forgives that too?"

Ann nodded. She knew his mother's story through Jade. She felt sorry for him and could relate to his pain. "Yes. Jesus died for her too. And she will receive that forgiveness only if she repents and believes in Him."

"Oh...then I am sorry to ask, what would your God say about the children who still hurt, the husband who was very hurt and he died in that pain. How does he justify the wrong done to them? Where is that justice for them?" His eyes were now blazing hot that Ann almost felt intimidated by them.

"The justice was done on Him, on Jesus. He was blameless. But He took your mother's and my stepfather's sins too on himself and bore their punishment all in advance. Only if they repent and believe they will receive that forgiveness. The same goes for all of us. Sin is sin. No big or small. All sin is equally sin for God." She said it with an assertion that came from experience.

"Okay, that's too much sin talk for a day. Let's go back to the room as I can see you are very sleepy." Phil changed the topic. It was getting too heavy for him and somehow her words were having a strange effect on his mind.

Ann sighed. She wanted him to feel God's love that helped her to forgive and move on so far in life. He too needed it so much. Well, at least she was able to speak to him about it. As they reached the hotel suite room, Ann bought the pillow and the extra quilt and gave Phil on the couch.

"I wasn't planning to sleep with you, Ms. Gomez...Not until tomorrow." He said the last words more to himself, smiling.

Ann heard it anyway having a sharp ear trained in the years for counseling. She came up to him. "Whatever did you mean by that? I hope you are joking."

Phil animated zipping his mouth and turned around and pretended to sleep smiling to himself. As Ann lay on the bed in the next room, she wondered what he meant even as a joke by 'not until tomorrow'?"

After an hour Phil was deep in his sleep when suddenly he was woken up by a whisper near his ears. "Come on Phil. Go up to her. She isn't a virgin anyways...she is already defiled...." It was a very coarse and deep voice, definitely not human.

Phil couldn't move at all. As if he was paralyzed on the couch. The voice continued, "You don't believe in God. That's good. He is a lie. There is nothing like sin. Go to her. Make her fail. Fall...Fall..."

Then there was silence. Phil felt his body free to move again. He got up with a jerk and looked around. There was no one there as the streetlights from out were giving enough light in the room to notice. Yet the voice was so very real. He went to Ann's bedroom. She was peacefully asleep. The Bible was in her hand. She must have fallen asleep while reading it.

He went to her, gently removed the Bible from her hand as he took it and went back to his couch. He kept thinking how did they manage to get to his mind? They had the dark power, he knew that. And this is what he was afraid was happening with Ann. But now they were playing games with his mind too. He sat on the couch and opened the Bible and right there staring at him was the verse:

Yea, though I walk through the valley of the shadow of death, I will fear no evil; For You are with me; Your rod and Your staff, they comfort me. Psalm 23:4

Was it a coincidence? Too much to be one. Ann's faith in God, does it hold true then? For why did it feel that the words were being spoken through the Book to him specifically? Because if there was so much supernatural darkness out there, then definitely what Ann talks of must be the supernatural light, he reasoned. All that he had believed in these years as an atheist that there is no God and that everything was in his control as he willed for it to be, it all seemed too petty before all this that was taking place now. The battle for a soul between the light and the darkness. He went back to reading the book further.

The next morning Ann was up and awake before Phil. She was very nervous about what he meant by "Not until tomorrow..." last night. Whatever surprise he had planned, it was scary now in context to what he had said. She quickly packed her backpack that she had got and wanted to silently move out. She was going back home. She had no intention to wait for him to give her a surprise to make her break her resolutions and then finding out he despised her after that for her phobia problem. She wasn't ready for that yet. No. Phil would have to marry her before he got close to her in that way. *So, let him come back and marry me if he loves me. I am not waiting for his surprise anymore.* She thought defiantly.

She moved out of the suite in a hurry not staying long enough on Phil to notice that he had fallen asleep reading her Bible. She was out on the street in no time. That early there was hardly anyone. It was the chill of autumn. She walked past some tourists having coffee to beat the cold. How she wished for a cup herself but there was no time to lose. Now, where would she find the bus or cab that would take her back to Orange County? She asked a person standing aside looking at the huge pond of water with the musical fountains she and Phil had been holding hands and watching last night. Oh, why did things have to get so complicated with Phil? They were having such a good time.

The person standing at the fountain area looked at her from top to bottom. He seemed very sinister Ann thought. But to her, all seemed that way. She still needed to stop judging people so quickly.

"So, can you tell me where I can find the bus or a cab to take me back to Orange County, California?"

She suddenly felt uncomfortable with him silently staring at her. Then she remembered she can check online for transport. In a hurry to get away before Phil realized, she forgot that. So, she hurriedly excused herself. "Thanks, don't bother...it's okay, I will manage."

"Wait." She heard him say and looked back at him.

He closed his dark greyish eyes for what seemed like forever. Then he suddenly opened them. Ann was shocked. His eyes had turned jet black with no visible iris and more like thin icy glass. Ann seemed to be drawn into them like a puppet. She couldn't run or even move by herself now. He turned and started walking away slowly and she followed him in a hypnotic trance. But this time her subconscious mind was alert inside her. Her bag fell off her shoulder as she just kept walking behind him. She wanted to pick up her bag but couldn't as she was strangely trapped within her own body. How she wished Phil were here to save her just this one more time. She prayed to God in her subconscious mind, even as she had no control over her body where ever it was being taken.

Phil was already on the streets desperately looking for her. When he got up, he saw that she was not in her room. She had left a message for him on his cell phone, "I am going back home to California. Don't come after me right now. I will not change my mind. I am not waiting to find out what you meant by 'Not until tomorrow' if that's your surprise. If you truly love me...come to my house and ask to marry me. Then I will go with you wherever you take me."

This reminded him of Jade just walking off leaving a note. "The foolish woman. Doesn't even know what's out there to get her." He muttered as he began almost running, looking around for her desperately.

A little ahead and he found her backpack lying on the ground. He picked it up and looked on all sides. Now she was in serious trouble. He had to find her and fast. He moved in the direction ahead asking passer-by's if anyone had spotted a young woman of Indian origin. All said no... then he all of a sudden had this soft voice in his head tell him to remember what he had read in the Bible the first time he opened it.

Yea, though I walk through the valley of the shadow of death...

The words resonated back to him again and again. He rushed towards the end of that street and asked two, three local people, if there was a valley nearby. They all said there wasn't any. He kept roaming each street like a mad man looking for a clue to find her. No, he couldn't lose her after coming so far. He couldn't bear the thought.

He just closed his eyes and said, "I know I said I would believe You existed if you made me find Jade. Which You did.... let me find just this one woman who is so precious to me. And she believes in You too. So will I... let me find her on time as a sign that You are listening to me."

It was desperate but genuine prayer from his heart for the first time in his life. As he frantically moved the streets, he came to a secluded path he felt compelled to go on. It ended towards an area like a plateau and a small valley kind of dip ahead in the plains. There, on the table-land kind of place where he stood, were some overgrown wild bushes and shrubs that were typical of the area and a huge old antique type of a gate rusted and with sculptures of vultures on both sides of the gate walls. *Very gothic in its design*, Phil thought. And above the gate on the metal arch for the name of the place, there was a very old rusty board half-fallen with the inscription on it, Dark Valley Resort! Valley. Dark...Shadow is dark too... Could this be the clue?

Phil saw that the gate was half-open. He entered cautiously looking around. The place had an eerie feel to it. There was a long driveway with neglected gardens on both sides of it full of overgrown shrubs and grass, unclean and dusty for years. *No one must have used this property for I don't know how long*, thought Phil. What if Ann wasn't here and he was wasting his time searching here for her just on a hunch? But then it was too good to be a coincidence that happened as soon as he had prayed for maybe the first time in his life, that particular verse came to his mind, and then he found this place.

He was lost in his thoughts when he was suddenly jolted out of them. Straight ahead of him at the end of the driveway, he saw Ann was walking on the parapet of the terrace of a four-story debilitated gothic style building. Phil could see she had no control over her actions as she looked as if in a trance. If he shouted for her she could fall with a shock. So, he silently went towards the building that must have been a gothic theme resort of some sort.

He climbed the steps at super speed. Even as he ran up the steps towards the terrace, he saw after reaching it, that towards the end of the terrace area opposite to him stood a man staring at him in a zombie-like state. He began to swiftly walk towards Phil even as Phil looked at Ann on the parapet and at him as to what action to take next. The man reached Phil faster than expected and he pushed Phil with a force that was not completely human. Phil went backward losing balance and fell towards the wall of the terrace. The man kept standing there staring in oblivion. Phil got up as he saw to his horror Ann was now walking on the parapet dangerously close to the edge with only a few inches between her and death.

Chapter 14

Phil saw that the crazy man shifted his glance at Ann now. He changed his direction towards her and began to walk fast in his zombie-like state in her direction to probably push her down the parapet. Phil had to move quickly, or the victory of evil was imminent. He saw a metal rod kept there with some junk metal stuff. He picked it up instinctively and ran ahead before the man could reach Ann.

Without making a sound Phil hit him on the back solidly. The man let out a loud cry. That seemed to break the hypnotic spell over him somehow. He seemed as if woken up from a deep sleep, "I ...what the hell...who are you...how did I get... here.... aah my back...it hurts..." he said and then he saw Ann on the parapet and the rod in Phil's hand. He understood something was amiss here and ran from there like he was in a marathon race.

Phil threw the iron rod aside and ran towards the parapet. Ann now stood in a position about to fall any moment. Phil moved quietly over the low wall separating the terrace and parapet. He had to be very careful. One wrong move could make him lose her forever. He slowly stretched his hand towards her left arm and as soon as he got the grip of it, he pulled her towards him with a jerk. She fainted instantly. He carried her over to the terrace taking deep breaths of relief.

Ann suddenly woke up in his arms and from the trance. He put her down and she caught her head as it was very heavy, looking at him. They didn't need words to explain to each other what was going on. She just hugged him tightly and cried. "I am sorry...I am so sorry..." she sobbed.

"It's okay, Ann. It's fine. Come, let's go." He said softly as he held her hands and they quickly walked out of that place.

****

That afternoon after resting a bit since both were exhausted and none spoke on the matter, Ann came to Phil and said, "I deserve what happened with me for not trusting you. From now on I do what you tell me to." Ann looked down as she said the last words meaningfully. She looked so endearing, like a little child caught in a naughty act.

"Good. So, start by getting fresh. Order lunch. I will be back in an hour." He said with the mocking attitude of a teacher.

Ann held his hand with tension. "Don't...leave me here alone."

Phil realized she was right. He couldn't take a chance anymore after almost losing her this morning. "Ok then. Get ready quickly. We will grab a bite out somewhere," he said.

"But where are we going, Phil?" Ann asked curiously.

"You Gomez people ask too many questions. It's a surprise, remember? Wait for it. Now be quick, will ya?" He said smiling warmly. There was no time to waste. Time was closing in on them.

Ann was excited about the surprise now. What happened today closed all doubts she ever had over Phil once and for all. She could see that he was sent by God for her protection from these strange forces that were beyond her comprehension. But she understood one thing, these strange happenings were related to those dark cult rituals she had been forced to be a part of in her childhood by Kevin O'Connor.

Ann got ready in no time. He asked her to wear a saree again, the Indian costume he found her looking gorgeous in. She had incidentally carried one as she knew he had admired her wearing it before. This was a light pastel peach butter crepe that gave a different glow to her skin. But she wondered why he insisted on a saree in the afternoon time. This was more a dinner type wear.

"Keep your driver's license, and passport with you." He told her. She wondered if they were going out of the country or what? Was that the surprise?

He was also ready in the same formal trousers and shirt he wore for the engagement. He was busy making some calls, but she couldn't hear the conversations as he was talking in a much lower tone. She put on very minimum makeup again and left her layered hair loose as usual. She managed to hear the end of the conversation he was having.

"Well, I hope all things are in place then as planned." She wondered what he meant by this and who was he talking to?

Once they were ready to leave, he finally noticed her in the saree again. She looked so beautiful. He just held her close with his one hand touching her waist on the open side of the saree. That sent ripples of sensation to her head. She closed her eyes and stood still.

"You are looking amazing, mermaid." He said softly near her ears with passion in his voice. He bought his lips down to hers. And there he stopped just before they could touch. She gasped with her mouth open a little as his grip on her waistline tightened even more as if it was helping him to control himself. Then, all of a sudden, the words of the strange voice last night reverberated in his mind.

"Go ahead...make her fail. Fall, Fall..."

It took all his strength for Phil to hold her hands and move out of the room abruptly. They sat in the car and Ann wondered, her mind still stuck near the door where he again almost kissed her but didn't. What was the matter? Will he ever kiss her? *Does he want to even?* Ann wondered.

He drove the car lost in his thoughts. Ann wondered what was he so deeply thinking about? Maybe about all the strange incidents happening with her. He broke the silence and said, somberly, "I read your Bible last night. A strange thing happened... I got the first verse, 'Even if you walk through the valley of the shadow of death....' even as I opened it and strangely when I err...prayed...yes for the first time in my life... I prayed to God to find you, that verse led me to you. The debilitated building where you were hypnotized or whatever today was once called Dark Valley Resort. I felt a voice say to me you are in there. And true enough you were."

Ann was shocked at his revelation and then smiled, thanking God within. "And so...now, do you believe there is God?" she asked hopefully.

Phil was silent for a moment before saying further, "I didn't just read that verse but a lot more especially the Gospel about Jesus and all the demon-possessed people he would set free at various instances, his other miracles, and sermons..."

"And so...?" this was getting exciting for her as it seemed like an answer to her prayers for him.

"I kind of... now believe... He is there... Yes...He is." He said still awkward by his confession. This was yet another new experience for him, thanks to Ann.

Ann just spontaneously hugged him tightly and kissed him on his cheeks. "Wow...wow," was all she managed in her joy. She so wanted him to also overcome his hurt feelings over his mother. And God could help him to do that. Just as He had helped her overcome her hatred of Kevin O'Connor. She didn't hate him anymore though she was unable to forget the memories that had more recently began to haunt her again and again.

Just then her phone rang. It was the Gomez's calling to ask how they were and where they were. As Ann excitedly told them where they were and how she was enjoying herself and then about Phil believing in God, Phil saw a childlike glee and innocence in Ann he hadn't seen in women of her age before, especially the joy when she spoke about him believing in God. As if she had her mission fulfilled. He saw that all that she had been through in her childhood couldn't kill the certain purity of her soul that was such an integral part of her personality. And he loved that uniqueness in her. Something had changed in him too for good because of her. Now just this one more thing was to ensure her safety and filling his mission.

On the way, he stopped the car at a busy shopping area. He asked her to sit in the car. He was back in twenty minutes. He got some sandwiches and her favorite cinnamon sticks to eat on the go. She wondered why there weren't sitting and eating at some joint? She was so dressed up too.

After driving some distance towards the outskirts of the city they came towards what seemed like a small hillock where he stopped the vehicle and they walked up the steps leading to a little Greek style wedding chapel called Agape Love. He looked at her deeply in her eyes as he held her hands tightly. She looked at him totally confused.

"We are getting married, Ann. Right here, right now. You can ask me all the questions later after this. Don't say anything else. Just say one word that matters now. Will you marry me? Yes or no?" he asked and waited.

Ann looked like she was frostbitten for a second. Then she smiled and said to her surprise said, "Yes, Phillip Jones, I will marry you and only you on this whole earth." Now she was more than ready. What exactly happened this morning, she wasn't so sure, but she was sure that she wanted Phillip Jones by her side for the rest of her life. He was God sent for her.

Phil was elated. The arrangements were already made in advance by him as this was the priority in the list of his plans. They entered the chapel, and the minister was already waiting to solemnize the wedding. Ann took permission from Phil to take her parents on the video call.

"Ann we will have one more ceremony in your church too. With all your folks and mine and hopefully Jade too by then." He assured her.

"Yes, but I want them to be a part of this first one also." She said excitedly. This was the best surprise ever and she was sure the Gomez couple would be happy for her more than anyone. She called them quickly and told them everything in short. They were first shocked beyond words, then Elena Gomez took over in full melodrama, the Gomez style. "Girl, your father is too possessive of you as all fathers are. But I say go for this one. He is a God-given answer to you, my Child. Don't lose this one. Oh, I am so happy for you both. Give him a kiss and a hug from our end. And yes, as you said we will plan a big fat wedding here too later. A Christmas wedding," she finished. Cristian Gomez grabbed the phone from her.

"My dear Ann. All I want is you to be a happy girl. Be blessed. You both have our blessings." He said emotionally. Ann was so happy.

Phil was getting restless. Any delay was calling for trouble right now after the incident this morning. Ann put the video call on, as Phil smiled and waved at the older couple. The minister began the wedding proceedings and finally, they both put the simple wedding bands he had purchased on the way for them on for each other's fingers and said the vows. Ann said, "I do," first. She had tears streaming down her cheeks. Phil wiped them with his fingers as he too said with full intensity looking into her moist eyes, "I do...."

The Gomez couple in the video call clapped their hands. Then as the minister said, 'you may kiss the bride' Phil took Ann in his arms without warning and kissed her before she could react. A full proper kiss, finally. Though Ann had longed for this all these days, right now she couldn't breathe and felt her heart would just pop out. For a second, she thought it was the panic attack happening again. But slowly as Phil guided her, she relaxed in his arms and kissed him back albeit quite awkwardly. Though it was a heady experience for him, for her this was the first time she was kissing someone in her lifetime. She shyly broke away as people were watching them.

Once they signed the register etc., they thanked the minister and left. Ann had put off the video call after the wedding and the wishing was over.

In the car, Phil seemed very serious as if he were focused on something ahead. Ann wondered what troubled him after such a happy event. She was herself in seventh heaven. She had got some good pictures clicked of them together as there was a chapel photographer ready there. She wished she had a wedding gown though instead of the saree. If only her 'ogre', she smiled, yes, now he was hers in every sense, if only he had shared his plan with her beforehand, she would have a nice wedding gown on, like every woman's dream. But it doesn't matter, in their family ceremony she will wear the best one ever, she told herself. They reached the hotel suite and Phil ordered room service dinner.

Once dinner was done, Ann suddenly felt apprehensive and restless. Will tonight be their wedding night too? This was to be that final test for her, she was very worried about. Phil on the other hand kept looking out of the room window. The danger had not yet passed away. Just one more thing needed to be done and that would be the final blow to their evil plans. And his avenging what they did to Jade. When he turned, he saw Ann looking at him questionably and he smiled and went up to her.

He moved her hair locks in a sensuous manner playing them with his fingers. She closed her eyes. As he looked her up, he moved closer to her face. "Open your eyes and look at me, mermaid. Look into my eyes," She looked up and what she saw in his eyes made her go weak in her knees. She began to stiffen up like a statue. He spoke close to her ear which was sensitive even to his warm breath as he said, "Mrs. Ananya Jones. Wow, sounds better still. But I must say, you are a bad kisser, you know, that right?"

Ann was shocked at first. She shyly shook her head no, as she said honestly, "I don't know. Haven't kissed anyone but you 'till date so how would I know." She said in a low voice.

Phil smiled, "But you taste heavenly..."

He said it putting his arms around her waist again sending her mind into a frenzy. She closed her eyes again. He knew he had to be extra gentle with her, especially after what she had been through. He carried her up in his arms and took her to the bedroom of the suite. Ann's heart was pounding. Now there were no excuses, no moral codes to be remembered, no limits that couldn't be crossed. But just her mind and the victory that had to be won there. She was nervous and could feel her breath getting heavier.

Her mind began to see pictures of her past with her stepfather Kevin, even those parts which she had tried to forget with great difficulty. The parts of the secret cult rituals and the sexual abuse later. They all seemed to come before her eyes now so that she couldn't focus on the romance or the handsome Phil before her eyes. For heaven's sake, he was now her husband. A man she loved more than her life. How does she tell him no tonight? Phil sensed her body turning cold and her breathing abnormal.

He understood and controlling himself said calmly, "Hey Ann, relax sweetheart, there is nothing that can't wait tonight. I want you to be at ease before I make love to you. And I so do want to..." He said with his voice heavy with desire.

Ann looked at him with gratitude in her eyes, "Thanks Phil. I don't know what to say...I.." she felt guilty.

"Just don't say anything... come let's dance..." he said pulling her out of the bed. Something to divert her mind and soothe her nerves at the moment.

He put on an old classic of Elvis Presley's, 'Can't help falling in love with you...' as he put his warm hand on her waist again through the saree. He loved how that felt.

Ann slowly relaxed and put her arms around his neck. This was so comfortable. *Will anything ever move forward than this for her? Or would the phobia eventually destroy what she has with Phil? Because how long can a man avoid something so important for him in a marriage?* Ann wondered as he put his face close to hers again.

Ann wanted him to kiss her again. So, she bought her face close to his, their lips almost touching. He was surprised at her move and confused too. He saw the desire in her eyes but knew she needed some time to be comfortable with him. So, he kept looking at her lips as he spoke in a voice deep with longing, "No. I can't kiss you here and not ... This can wait." He said and moved away a bit. He knew this had to be done for her good and to bring the evil's plans to nothing. But he couldn't hurt Ann and do it.

Ann was disappointed as he had moved away. What did she want? She was confused at her mixed feelings right now. Then Phil patted her face, almost like a sister she felt and took his pillow and quilt to the living room couch. Ann sighed. What an end to a great day. She cried herself to sleep that night praying, "Oh God why couldn't I relax? Why couldn't I just allow things to flow?"

Phil was happy as he lay on the couch. She belonged to him now and nothing could change that, though if the marriage were not consummated, the danger that lurked over her would not yet pass. He was confident that once in his home at Carson City, she will be more comfortable, and things will fall into place. It was a matter of one more day. That was his next surprise for her. With this satisfaction, he fell asleep.

Chapter 15

Next morning Ann was woken up with the sunlight falling on her face from between the window curtains. She saw Phil standing there with his back to her looking out. She kept staring at his back. He was bare-chested with only his boxers on. She could see his body was athletic with broad shoulders and chest and a narrow waistline. She admired him dreamily.

Phil was lost in his thoughts. There were secrets about him that Ann didn't know yet. The biggest one being that he had once been a part of the secret cult that Ann's stepfather Kevin O'Connor belonged to. He came to know that after he read her diary. He had a mission earlier to get to those bastards who had destroyed his sister Jade's life to teach him a lesson for leaving their cult. But he was fearless of them and that's where they had no hold on him. They played on people's fears. And then he decided to avenge Jade.

When he got close to Ann's past, he knew what they would do to her as per the rules of their cult. And then Ann didn't know it, but her stepfather Kevin O'Connor, who was now one of the many cult masters, was out from prison too. That's when Phil decided what he had to do both for Jade and Ann's sake. He had already conquered the first half of his mission with the wedding and given them a solid blow. They must be fuming over his audacity to defy them. They never take such things lying down, especially from people who were once part of them. And in this he and Ann both had a common ground.

Ann sighed. *Oh, if only I was a normal person. I could make you the happiest man on earth Phil.* She thought to herself. Even as she was imagining romantic things about him, Phil turned suddenly as he caught her shutting her eyes at once and pretending to be asleep. He smiled and came close to the bed and stood. She could smell his musky fragrance near her. He looked at her naughtily and snuggled in bed under the quilt with her. She stiffened up at the proximity of his body.

He just bought his face closer to her on the pillow at the side. "Hey, beautiful. Good morning. I want to thank you for trusting me the way you did with the sudden plans for the chapel wedding. Anyone else in your place would have gone insane. I shall be ever grateful to you all my life, love." He said it with so much emotion that Ann opened her eyes in surprise to see him. She smiled and blushed. He was grinning at her.

"Tricked ya..." He chuckled. Then suddenly his face became serious as he asked looking straight into her eyes, "Do you love me Ananya Jones?" he asked with the funny accent he said Ananya with. Ann was speechless for a moment.

She had never said that to any man ever before other than her adoptive dad Cristian. But that was different. Then with all the emotions, she was capable of she said, "I ...I love you...Phillip Jones...more than I ever have in my life and ever will...I love you." She closed her eyes with this so he wouldn't see the tears that formed so easily in her eyes from the intense emotion she felt. But one drop came out like a rogue from the corner of her eye. Phil took it on his finger as he looked at it in the sunlight that came through the window.

"Precious. Everything about you is precious to me." Then he looked at her with intense passion as he came close to her and took her in his arms and kissed her on her forehead. This was a good way to get her to be comfortable with him. By experience, he knew women needed to be emotionally secured before the physical part. And with Ann it was imperative.

Ann lay on his chest savoring that moment as if it wouldn't come back if she moved away. While lying there she asked him without having to look at him. "Phil, why did you marry me so suddenly as a surprise? You said I could ask such questions after we are married. We were anyways engaged weren't we and you had permission to take me along?"

Phil was at a loss for words. He couldn't tell her yet. Not until the final requirement is fulfilled. "Well, I couldn't keep my hands off you Madame, and each time I came closer, Mr. Gomez's face would flash before me saying, 'limits, limits, limits'," he said jokingly. But it wasn't a lie either. Just not the complete truth.

Ann smiled and hit him on the chest playfully. Thanks to her dad's warning, whatsoever, she was his wife now. And she was loving it.

They checked out that afternoon. After lunch at the restaurant below, they left for Carson City.

"Now this is the second part of my surprise for you, the place where we are going to," he said.

Ann was a happy woman even if he took her to the remotest part of the earth. As long as he will be there with her. God had finally made a way for her to be set free from the dark shadows of her past by sending Phil Jones into her life.

Phil on the other hand was more in a somber mood as he drove his vehicle. He was cautious about the danger that still lurked over their heads. He had only won half the battle and they must be planning something big to get even. *The monsters*, he fumed to himself. There was so much in him that he wanted to share with somebody but couldn't trust anyone and he couldn't tell Ann just yet. Gradually he would have to but telling her about his secret right now would devastate her and create a lot of unwanted misunderstandings between them which would eventually thwart all he had planned so far. He would have to wait for the right time.

As of now, all he wanted was to introduce Ann to his younger brother Jeff and his family who lived close to his house but more in the main part of Carson City. And then he wanted to carry Ann across the threshold of his own home. Now their home. It felt strange to say that.

After divorcing Sarah, Phil never bought any of his subsequent girlfriends' home. He thought he was in love with Sarah. She was a gorgeous woman alright. But everything finished the day he caught her red-handed with one of his close buddies in their bedroom. Then there was a Pandora of other things that came out. Phil was devastated. It kills a man to think he is not enough for his woman. Later after the divorce, he had an affair with his childhood friend Michelle in rebound and also to spite Sarah, but it didn't last long and there was no emotional commitment from both sides. He never took Michelle home, ever. But Ann was not only his wife now, but she was also special. Very special.

They entered Carson City. It was a beautiful place and a part of Lake Tahoe, where he had their restaurant. It was hardly half an hour from there Phil told her. They would go there soon too. Phil took Ann first to his brother's place. Ann was pleasantly surprised, first, to be in his hometown, and then, to meet his rather reserved brother Jeffery, who was chubbier and had a small beard and moustache. *But he was also tall like Phil and his wife Rudy was tall too, around 5"9' maybe*, thought Ann. She was a slim and pretty blonde American woman a couple of years older than Ann.

She didn't look like she was a mother to a three-year-old kid because she was fit as a fiddle. They both got along like a house on fire. Little Jamie, that was the name of their three-year-old, was a bundle of mischief and got along wildly with her uncle Phil. Ann could see him play with her and her heart warmed up to him. He would surely be a great father. But then a dark shadow again overshadowed her happy thoughts. What if she failed to give Phil that happiness? That would be so unfair to him after what happened with him and his ex-wife.

"You will have dinner with us...please, and why don't you stay back here today?" Rudy asked Ann keenly breaking her thoughts.

"No Rudy, not today. But someday soon." Phil butted in almost immediately. "Ann needs to see our home." Ann felt warm the way he said it, 'Our home'.

Jeff seemed a bit aloof from Ann all evening but was fond of his brother Phil a lot. Maybe he was unhappy with Phil's choice of a bride, her being of a different culture and race to theirs? Maybe he expected Phil to marry an American or a European blonde or red head. She saw Jeff talk heatedly with Phil over something in the garden area. Ann was trying to make friends with Jamie. But probably she was a stranger to her and so she would take time to get used to her. After a while, Phil came in and said, "Ann, you stay here tonight. I have urgent work to resolve. I will be back by tomorrow morning to take you."

Ann felt sad. She so wanted to go to their house. And she wanted to start living a normal life with him. She wanted to be the normal woman in Phil's life. But she can afford to have patience she thought, after all, she had decided to trust Phil without questions. She nodded a half-hearted yes and Phil left giving her a peck on her cheek. Well, at least she had Rudy to bond with. She seemed to be a simple woman from a smaller town who yearned for company in her age group. Jeff didn't seem a man who would spend much time romancing his wife. That way Phil was much more a romantic and thankfully so. Because whether Phil knew it yet or not, in her heart Ann was a diehard romantic.

As Ann went to get fresh in the guest room given to her for the night, she couldn't help but wonder where Phil had to go so urgently. She made some urgent calls back home to her parents and some colleagues who were also friends, enquiring about any news on the Clara Smith case and the girl who disappeared the other day during their dinner at the fine dining restaurant. As for Clara Smith, there was no clue yet. But the girl at the restaurant was found the very next day. And strangely her memory seemed to have been wiped out for she knew nothing of who those people were and where she was taken, as per the girl's description. She had however not been harmed. Ann felt uneasy. Could it be the same people Jade wouldn't disclose much about out of fear back then? *That was a possibility,* Ann told herself.

Phil reached his home a little away from the main city, a huge two-storied house facing a lake a little far away from it as the house itself was on a tiny hillock. The lake had boats tied up near it of owners and people who hire out. Phil had one of his own too. Phil got out of his car clenching his jaws. Jeff had told him that there was a visitor at his place, Sarah, his ex-wife. She had called Jeff and told him she was going to stay at Phil's as she still had an extra key and was in town for a couple of days for some urgent work.

She was from Los Angeles and had returned after the divorce. Jeff had always been fond of Sarah and never wanted the divorce to happen. Sarah had a way of making all-male species be attracted to her no matter what, sexual or asexual. Phil opened the door with a jolt. He was very angry. What the heck! At least she could have the courtesy to call and inform him. This was no longer her home. She had lost that right the day she decided to have those clandestine affairs of hers. The divorce was just a formality. He entered the house, but she wasn't there, downstairs, anywhere. He could hear soft music playing upstairs.

"Now don't tell me she is having a good time with someone in my bedroom again. I will kill her." Phil muttered under his breath. He went up the staircase and true enough the music was coming from his bedroom with the door left a bit open and not from the adjoining one.

"The insolent woman...." he said and opened the door of his room. Sarah was in there swaying to the seductive song playing on a portable speaker, with just a towel wrapped around her and she was about to dry her hair with a dryer. She looked at Phil pretending to be shocked and embarrassed. Her towel was about to slip so she held it tightly to herself.

"Oh, Phil. You frightened me. Well, I am sorry. I heard you were out of town, so I decided to stay for a couple of days here. Hope you don't mind. I have some urgent work in Carson tomorrow."

Phil stood a bit perplexed. Why did this woman still affect him? The song that was playing was also the one they would listen to on their romantic nights together. Maybe it was the song that was bringing back those unwanted memories. Even though he wanted to give her a piece of his mind, he couldn't bring himself to be rude to her. Some of their good times together were spent here in this very bedroom. Oh, why did she have to come here? Not now. No.

"Err...well can you please shift to the guest room down? I want my room. My wife Ann is here with me in Carson. I will be bringing her here tomorrow morning."

Sarah's face darkened though she pretended to be happy for him, "Hmm, yeah, Jeff told me. I don't mind I was so used to this bathroom, so I...." She said adjusting her towel. Phil felt awkward when she did that. Some years back she would have come over without that towel and seduced him here in this room. He violently brushed the whole memory aside.

"Can I use the adjoining room if you don't mind? It's also similar to this one." She asked trying to sound genuine. That was the room they had planned for their kid when they would have one. Phil didn't like her playing these games with his mind. He wanted to get her out of his sight, so he didn't argue with her and he said hurriedly. "Yes. Please move your stuff there right away. And how long do you plan to stay?"

Sarah fluttered her eyes. She knew that used to be his weakness when they were together. *Men were such suckers when it came to the power of a woman who was confident of her sexuality*, Sarah thought. "Hardly two days more." She said smiling and showing off her milky whites. Sarah was a woman so sure of herself and her body language spoke oodles of sensuality, which she was good at manipulating with, Phil knew that well enough. Phil nodded and moved down to the living area. He was already missing Ann.

Ann couldn't sleep again thinking of Phil. She wanted to be with him right now. It was a new place, and she was still not used to it. She called his cell once, but he didn't answer. Maybe he was very busy. He would tell her tomorrow whatever it was. She decided to write a poem about her fantasy with Phil. Of how it would be for her when they will come together for the first time. She took her diary and began to write.

Dear Diary,

There was a darkness so dense that surrounded me, it threatened to engulf me into the fire of Hell,

But then I believed in the light that has taught me not to be afraid or on my dark past to forever dwell.

From that light I saw this knight come riding on a white stallion towards me, sweeping me off my feet.

Away from that dense darkness and then in his arms, I let myself be, savoring his breath so sweet...

He moved the locks off my face and that touch sent ripples of fiery liquid in all my senses, And then he...

Even as she was about to write further, she heard footsteps outside her door where there was a lamp burning. The footsteps moved to the left then to the right. Then it stopped in front of her door. She got a bit paranoid. Who could it be here in Jeff's house? Suddenly there was a shuffling sound near her window. It was the first floor so probably it came from down. She swallowed hard as she moved towards the window slowly to look down and she saw a black dark figure disappear in the darkness beyond the garden area outside. Was she hallucinating all this? She promised herself she was going to see a psychiatrist soon. But Ann's heart began beating fast as she looked at the door of the room.

The knob began to move slowly as if someone was trying to open it. Her breathing became erratic. She looked around the room and found a stick kept aside for the fireplace. She picked it and quickly went behind the door. The room was dark except for the garden lamp light coming in from the window. The door slowly opened and there was a man who entered in. Ann took the lead and hit him hard on the head with the stick and the man caught his head with a loud cry. She was proud of herself today as she felt a surge of courage come into her. She rushed to switch on the light but before she could do that the man was quicker and he pushed her to the wall and put his hand on her mouth before she could scream. In the little light of the room, she saw it was Phil.

He smiled and said, "That was some show of courage, Mrs. Jones. I liked this new move of self-defense." He said grinning as he left her mouth free.

"I ...I am so sorry ...Phil... I." She said embarrassed. Should she tell him about the dark figure down near the garden? No. He will think she is losing her mind.

"It's ok, sweetheart. I want you to be alert like this. It's important." He said in context to the danger he was aware of.

Ann took hold of herself and said, "I want to see the clout on your head. I think it was bad. Let me..." before she could move to put on the light Phil suddenly held her close and kissed her without warning. This time it was a full passionate kiss. At first, Ann tensed up a bit, but then she relaxed in his grip and let him guide her to it. Her mind was as if floating in the air, around those pine trees where their attraction first began.

It felt as if the stars were twinkling in the dark sky and the moon shining above their heads. She felt poetry at this moment. He smelled and tasted heavenly she realized now that she was calm in his arms. After some time when he lifted his head away from her, she was breathless and smiling. Before he could say anything further, this time she kissed him back again, and then again.

Finally, he said, "Whoa, Mrs. Jones. Are you planning a lifetime in a day?"

Ann smiled. She felt liberated. As if in one part of her mind something was set free like a bird out of a cage. "I think I can do that forever..." She laughed happily.

"Well, get some sleep, will ya? Because I am taking you home tomorrow. And there I plan to make you mine forever." He said it meaningfully, but this time there was this little uncertainty in him because of Sarah's unwanted presence in the house.

She slept well snuggled in his arms. She was smiling to herself with her head pressed against his chest. Finally, they had kissed. The way Britney had said couples do. This was sure a good start because right now she felt no palpitations, no heavy breathing, no panic attack at all. Just plain bliss.

Phil was a bit tensed now that Ann couldn't see his expressions. He came away here because though Sarah had shifted to the next room to his, he somehow didn't trust what she was up to. Her body language was strange he felt. Also, he would have to tell Ann in the morning about her being there in the house. He hoped Ann would take it well.

Chapter 16

They reached Phil's house in the afternoon after having a great breakfast that Rudy and Ann prepared together. She got to know from Rudy what Phil loved to eat. She planned to make those dishes once at their place. Phil told her everything about Sarah's being at his place last night on the way while driving. She seemed a little taken aback at first but later was cool about it.

"I trust you, Phil. I know you are long over her. Now you are mine." She had said squeezing his arms tightly.

Phil smiled awkwardly. He hadn't told her about that moment when he saw Sarah in a towel and the song that was playing on her mobile, that it all did unsettle him a bit and brought back memories. He felt some things were better unsaid.

As they approached the front porch, Ann was busy looking around while Phil wondered if Sarah would be there. She had said she had work around town, so probably she won't be there. That would be such a relief because it would give him time to help Ann to feel at home without any unwanted awkwardness. The house had a huge lawn and a flower garden before the porch. Ann loved the house and the surroundings. Just like the one in her dreams, she thought.

As they walked towards the house Ann was suddenly pulled down by a huge golden retriever dog who pounced on her from nowhere. Phil ran towards her and the dog left Ann and was all over Phil licking him like mad. Ann understood this must be Phil's dog whom he forgot to mention to her. Ann loved dogs too. But never got to keep one because Elena was allergic to them. Then suddenly Ann saw a tall slender woman approach from behind the dog. She was a classic American beauty. With dark blonde hair and green eyes. Ann understood this must be Sarah who called out to the dog, "Gorgeous, Gorgeous, come here my poodle."

And Gorgeous obeyed and began to her wag her tail.

Phil looked disappointed. Why was she still here and with Gorgeous too? Who asked her to bring the dog here?

"Hey Phil, I missed you in the morning. When did you leave last night?" She asked giving him a peck on his cheek. Ann's mouth fell at that.

Phil was visibly uncomfortable with her around. "Why have you got Gorgeous here? She is doing well with Rob. He takes good care of her." He asked vehemently.

Sarah looked at Ann from top to bottom and said, "Well won't you introduce me to your... wife, I guess?" She asked almost purring her words out.

Phil introduced Ann to her without a smile. "Ann, this is my ex-wife Sarah, and this is my wife, Ananya Jones." He emphasized the surname.

Ann said a plain, "Hi...", while Sarah said, "Hello there...", with panache.

Gorgeous once again started jumping over Ann. She had instantly taken to her it seemed.

"Oh, stop it, Gorgeous. She is very fond of Phil. You must be carrying his scent." She said sarcastically looking at Phil while saying the rest, "She was bought by Phil and me when we were courting. It was kind of a bonding factor back then." Sarah concluded with a strange note in her tone.

Phil just looked away and muttered sarcastically, "Didn't help much, did it? Now if you will excuse me, I have very important work to discuss with my wife. Please drop Gorgeous back at Rob's, will you?" Saying this curtly he just took hold of Ann's hand and moved inside.

Ann was a bit surprised. Sarah still affected him, in the sense of getting him angry and worked up. That is also an emotion. Well, looking at Sarah it wasn't a surprise. She was drop-dead gorgeous to start with and had that oomph factor in plenty. Ann felt she could never fit into that description, ever. That wasn't her. What if Phil desired women of Sarah's kind? Wouldn't she be too simple and out of the league to keep him interested in her all his life?

"Take one day at a time Ann... relax." She told her self-talking a deep breath.

"A penny for your thoughts?" Phil asked her as he picked her up in his arms at the main door on the porch and bought her inside. He put her down and closed the door behind them as he took her in his arms and then started playing his lips around her ears and hair at the side of her face. Ann could feel her entire body and breath on fire suddenly. She looked at him. His eyes took away all her doubts and fears for the moment. He looked at her with a cocktail of love, desire, and passion. She wouldn't stop him now or ever, Ann thought.

Phil had Sarah still at the back of his mind somewhere and he wanted to get rid of her as soon as possible. He took Ann up to his room and closed the door. Ann looked around pretending to see the interiors whereas her heart was beating way too fast she felt. Her head was dizzy with anticipation of what would it be when he... As if he read her thoughts, he caught her hands and swirled her close to him. She felt like she was putty in his hands. He kissed her deeply and passionately and she reciprocated with the same desire.

I think now is the time. She seems ready. There isn't time to waste anyway. They haven't made any significant move for some time. Would mean they are planning something big. Phil thought to himself. He lifted her in his arms and carried her to the bed. As he was about to put her down, he suddenly exclaimed, "What the heck?!"

He put Ann down on the ground again as he went over the bed and picked up the photos that lay scattered around on it. Ann also picked up a couple of them. They were Sarah and Phil's pictures of the wedding and the celebration later. And she saw some still lying on the bed and picked them up. They were some very intimate pictures of Sarah and him kissing and a few of Sarah posing semi-nude while Phil must have clicked her. Ann felt a strong jab of jealousy pierce her insides. It was long back and was his past, but she couldn't help feeling the anger rise in her.

"What are these doing on your bed, Phil? Were you seeing your wedding album with Sarah yesterday?" She asked with indignation.

Phil was at a loss for words. This was the witch Sarah's work after he had left for Jeff's last night. "Well, this is her work alright. I have a feeling Sarah still thinks she stands a chance with me again." Phil said honestly between his teeth.

"I thought so too. But may I ask you something? After all this time why have you kept this album with you still?"

Phil looked at Ann. Jealous women can ask too many questions he thought. "I was going to dispose of it once I was back home. Remember, I am coming back home with you for the first time since we met?"

Ann realized that is true. She wondered if all these years since their divorce did Phil sit and look at these and remember his times with Sarah, especially the intimate pictures? She couldn't bear the thought. "I will get lunch ready for us. You relax and err...get rid of...all this." She said trying hard to sound casual. All these feelings were new to her. She was just learning to deal with them. Right now, she couldn't help feeling disturbed.

"Ann... come here." He pulled her close to him again. She tried to look away. But she pulled her face up to look at him. Her eyes were moist much to her embarrassment.

"Hey, love. I know what you are thinking. I am sorry about her being here. It was so unexpected. She will be gone in a day or two. Don't be insecure, ok? What I feel for you is a level even you can't understand right now."

Ann smiled shyly. She believed him and said cheering up in a good mood again, "Well, all said and done. We still need lunch. And you have a certified legal cook for it as of now, me." She smiled as she remembered Rudy filling her with details of his favorite dishes.

Phil smiled with warmth. This was one woman he was determined to keep all his life.

After a tasty lunch that day, where Sarah was missing, Phil decided to show Ann around his property, and also, he would dispose of the album of pictures in the fireplace that night, he thought. Sarah must have gone on her business for which she said she was here.

As they moved around the property with Ann holding on to his arms, she was amazed at actually how vast it was. Phil and Jeff owned a ranch too with some great stallions in the lot. They stopped over at Rob's cottage close to the ranch who was a friend to their father and a caretaker of Phil's property. He was also a farmer by profession. He was a very cute and warm old man around sixty-five years of age, more like a father figure for Phil.

Phil told Ann before they came to see him that he remained unmarried because the woman he loved was married off elsewhere. He never could love anyone so much again to lead to the alter. He lived with his nephew John who also helped him on the ranch with other helpers who came and went. Rob liked Ann instantly and it was mutual. He told her Phil was crazy about horses and was more into the ranch and Jeff would be busier into the Jones restaurant they owned nearby and wanted to expand its joints in other places too.

"I am happy for you, Phil. Your dad would have been so happy to see you with Ann. Now we can expect some cute little ones playing about your backyard too." He laughed.

Ann blushed and smiled, looking away. Phil looked at her expectantly and said, "I would love that too."

"Well, Sarah was here this morning and took Gorgeous with her. Then she took John with her downtown and Gorgeous too for a bit of grooming."

Phil tensed at the mention of her name. Was she now eyeing John, Rob's nephew, who was a couple of years younger than Phil and quite handsome himself? Why should it matter to him? Phil chided himself.

"You must keep that one away from your home and marriage Phil. She hasn't changed a bit. As selfish as ever." Rob advised as an elderly man who had seen more life than them.

"I will keep that in mind Rob. Thanks. I want to take Ann for a ride to the boating club of the lake. I hope our boats are in good shape?" Phil asked as Jeff also owned one for himself.

"Sure, go ahead. Just got them serviced last week." Rob said.

Within an hour, Phil and Ann were on the motorboat and having a great ride around the lake. Ann loved the feel of the plain mountains and faraway snow peaks. Winter would set in soon and there was a chill even as the sun shone brightly. It was a beautiful place but the question that Phil and Ann hadn't discussed yet as if she came to live here, what about her profession as a counselor? There wasn't much for her out here in that context. Well, she didn't want that to spoil what she had right now. In time they will discuss that too.

She was suddenly jolted out of her thoughts as the boat stopped abruptly with the motor sputtering because the boat wasn't moving forward. They were in the middle of the lake with the shore quite far away. And Phil had told her it was a deep lake. Ann shuddered as she hadn't learned swimming what with being so involved in resolving the other issues of her life.

"Shucks! Rob said it was serviced. Then how come this?" Phil said with a surprised tone.

He got to check the motor of the boat. It was absolutely fine and working. *What could be the issue?* Phil thought. He looked down into the dark water. Maybe something stuck below the boat was stopping it from moving ahead. The water was chilly though with the sun still up it wouldn't be unbearable, and Phil was used to these parts since his childhood. He took off his shirt and denim as he said, "I need to go down and check on this one. There is something stuck down there."

Ann was terrified as she said, "Phil, the water. It's deep and... scary...don't. Can't we call someone for help?"

"Hey, trust me, I know these parts like the back of my hand. Don't worry at all. There's anyway no range out here for the cell phones." He assured her.

She checked her cell and his. It was true. The range of the network was almost zero. Phil took a deep breath before jumping into the lake and disappearing underneath the boat. Ann looked into the lake and all she could see was the reflection of her face in the dark water. She kept staring into the lake to see a sign of Phil when suddenly she saw a face come out of the water looking at her. It was Kevin O'Connor's face staring with his eyes wide open into hers and she felt drawn into them like a moth to the fire. As she felt herself lose control of her body, the face disappeared into the water and she felt herself fall into the lake without any control or sense of what was happening.

She could feel herself go down in the dark water beneath and due to a little sunlight coming in from above she saw Kevin O'Connor's face and body parallel to hers going down with her. He was talking to her as if in telepathy, "Foolish girl. You thought you could escape me. Nor your God, nor your man, can save you now. You belong only to me. And now you will belong to him forever."

There was no struggle, no movement in her body at all. All those flashbacks of those rituals that she was forcibly initiated into in her childhood came back to her in detail right now. How she was made to sit in a semi-drugged state before their ugly demon god's image and she was surrounded in a circle by those hooded men and women with strange masks on their faces. How a piece of her hair was cut and taken and then finally the blood covenant with their cult and the devil himself. But amid all these dark flashbacks came the brightest ray of light,

"You are my hiding place; you will protect me from trouble and surround me with songs of deliverance" (Psalm 32:7)

Ann was suddenly reminded of the verse she had read so many times in the Holy Bible. She remembered the Lord and the many times he had protected her 'till now, even though Phil, and suddenly, she was set free from the hypnotic state, she was drowning in right that moment. There was no sign of Kevin O'Connor there anymore. Now fully conscious she struggled to get back on top as she had sunken quite deep down but not touched bottom yet as it was a very deep lake. She could feel her lungs parched now for oxygen and anytime she would swallow water within. She didn't know how to pull herself back upwards. Well, this was it then.

"See you, Lord, in Heaven," she thought in her mind.

All of a sudden, a hand-pulled her t-shirt upwards and she came face to face with Phil. *Oh thank you, Lord*, she thought. But was it too late? She had started swallowing water within and could feel her inner parts fill up. Phil desperately moved fast to get her to the top.

When he had come up to the boat after inspecting it underneath and finding no reason for it to have stopped, he found Ann missing and jumped in again to search for her. Now finally he got her to the top and after catching up with his breath he realized she had stopped breathing. No. God. Not now. Not after bringing them so far. He put her into the boat with a bit of a struggle and got in himself and tried to pump out the water from her stomach by turning her on the back. She lay still down in the boat. He then did the mouth-to-mouth resuscitation and waited. No response. Then he repeated until finally she sputtered water out of her mouth and began to breathe again. Phil now just plunked himself backward in the boat with relief and fatigue. Ann felt like she was given a new life. She got up slowly feeling a little odd inside still and looked at Phil who smiled at her lying where he was.

"I... sorry Phil. I saw him again in the lake. Kevin O'Connor. He seemed to draw me with those eyes... believe me, it's no hallucination... he's doing it...I can't understand how....because he is supposed to be in prison..." her voice choked with emotion before she could say anything more.

Phil got up and took her into his arms. "Shh don't...Ann... just relax okay? Don't say a word. I think God truly loves you. He always sends me on the right time." After she had calmed down, he started the motor of the boat and the boat moved forward to his relief.

This is it. Tonight, he had to do what had to be done. There were no second thoughts to that. And he would allow neither her past nor his to stop him this time.

Chapter 17

After Ann's nerves had settled down and she was warm and tucked under the quilt, Phil kissed her on the head and said, "I'm going to the main city square and will be back in a jiffy. I have some important work to finish. And I need to get us dinner too. So, don't worry about doing that." Ann nodded, smiling warmly. The incident had shaken her up badly within. This time things had gone too far. She just snuggled into the quilt and tried to have a small power nap 'till Phil would be back.

Phil knew what he was going to do. He was going into town to get some good wine, flowers, and chocolates. And some good dinner too. He was going to have a candlelight dinner set up for them. Just the things to relax and calm Ann down for the special moment tonight. Sarah had come in earlier when Ann was having a warm bath prepared by Phil. She didn't bother to check on them or come out of her room and Phil liked it that way.

Right now, Ann had fallen into a neutral sleep with no dream or nightmare this time. Just plain nothing, thankfully. She didn't remember how long she must have dozed off when she was woken up by her cell phone ringing. It was Phil's call, "Hey hottie mermaid, hope you are fine. Just checking on you. Don't doze off for the night. I have something planned for us. I want you to be as relaxed as possible."

He said with a voice that suddenly made a pang of desire to hit her as she understood his connotation behind the words. "Yes...I am waiting." She said with as much passion to match. She surprised herself. Phil surely bought out in her more than she could ever imagine. Suddenly there was a knock on her door and her heart skipped a beat. Who could it be? Was it Phil giving her a surprise? The knock came again. Ann didn't say a word. She wanted to call Phil right away when suddenly the door opened and there stood Sarah, looking as ravishing as ever in a red evening dress with a plunging neckline almost down to her upper waist. Ann never had the guts to go that wild with her dressing. Maybe because she didn't desire unwanted male attention her way. Was Sarah dressed to kill someone today? Maybe Phil?

"Hey. Are you alright? Just wanted to check. You are looking quite pale." She said with more concern than suited her personality.

Ann was cautious as she said, "Yes...I am fine. Thank you."

"I saw Phil leave in a hurry half an hour back. So? How's it going with him? He can be a darling and so difficult at the same time." She chuckled the words out.

Ann felt a bit nervous talking to her. With years of training in counseling, she could note that the woman was hinting at something else.

"He can be a great husband but is quite a demanding one let me warn you. Especially in bed." She said unabashedly.

Ann swallowed hard. What was she up to?

"Look I don't want to scare you, just want you to know something which maybe he hasn't told you and never will. He is a part of the secret cult that your stepfather Kevin O'Connor belongs to. He told me that himself last night," she said and stopped, letting that sink into Ann. Ann was numb for a moment. Sarah continued, "During our married days he would come home with those weird thoughts and ideologies he would learn there in their strange rituals which I got to know eventually consists of wild sexual orgies and drugs of all kinds. He wanted me to be a part of them. I refused point-blank. So, he started mistreating me. I tried pleasing him in all his sexual demands. But it was never enough. As if sex was almost diabolical for him. That's when I got attracted to a less complex friend of his. And rest is history," she finished, looking pleased with herself the way she put it across.

Ann was flabbergasted. Things started falling into place about Phil suddenly, the way he turned up every time to help her from that first day at the warehouse. Then he always seemed to know about what she is going through. He also seemed quite cool about the paranormal activity happening around them and especially with her.

Sarah continued further, "If you haven't noticed, he still is quite attracted to me and gets affected by my presence. That's the amount of sensuality we shared. I don't think any woman can ever give him that. Last night I was in the towel when he entered the bedroom. I was looking at our old album when he also came and sat next to me looking at our intimate pictures. The look in his eyes said it all to me. He then kissed me quite wildly you know as if he was..." She was saying it all sensuously as if she was as madly in love with Phil when Ann just cut her off.

"Please...stop...I... I don't want to...hear anything...more." Ann said fully drained out of energy.

The tears just streamed down Ann's eyes without control. She felt she couldn't breathe. Phil? The only man she ever trusted her soul with. The only man she ever loved. He was a part of all that evil happening to her. And he already cheated on her with... No, this isn't happening. It's a bad dream.

"Can you just.... leave me alone... please." Ann managed to say to her in a choked voice.

Sarah said without much emotion, "Sorry about that. I wouldn't want any woman's life ruined as mine was. So, I said what I said. If you tell him that I told you all this, then get ready to see his violent side. He might just kill me. Also, if you wait to confront him, he will hypnotize you and make you do what he wants and go where he wants as he must have been doing all this while without you knowing it. You must have been seeing hallucinations too which is also his doing. Tell me haven't strange things been happening to you since he met you? Well, I know all this because I have experienced it all." With this, she walked out.

Ann was now stuck big time. No, she couldn't stay back there to confront him. Not after what Sarah said at the end of her revelation. Ann couldn't take a chance. She needed to leave as soon as possible from here. But how? What about transport? She checked online. There were private car rentals available to take her back home. They were expensive at this hour, but she was ready to spend a fortune if necessary, to get away from this man. She spoke to one of the car rental companies that were reputed there and booked a car. It was expected in half an hour. She just prayed Phil wouldn't come before that. Her mind was going crazy and numb at the same time.

"Why dear Lord. Why me?" she cried. She packed in a hurry and went down to wait for the car. Sarah was in her room and didn't come out. Ann was in a way grateful to her for bringing the truth out. But she was as complicated as Phil and they both deserved each other Ann thought with sadness in her heart.

"Anyways he needs a sensual woman like Sarah who can match up to his appetite for lust. Not a nervous wreck like me," she said to herself. She got a call from the rental car driver in a little more than half an hour that seemed like a lifetime right now. He was out in the driveway. Ann just picked her two bags quickly as she was anyways traveling light. Once in the car, she gave a last look at the house feeling emotional that she had thought this would be her home forever. As her cab left from the driveway to the main gate Phil entered in his vehicle wondering who could have come at this hour. He had got delayed as the florist had closed. He managed somehow because he had contacts and got them to give him Ann's favorite flowers. He had read in her diary that she loved the day lily that bloomed only for a day. Because she believed nothing here (on earth) is forever. But he wanted her to believe their love is forever and he would make sure of that.

Ann was crying all through the way. She kept wiping her tears, but they immediately came back again. The driver was a middle-aged man who kept looking at her through the rear mirror. She kept remembering every moment spent with him and also the fact that now she understood why would an attractive, well to do American man who had gorgeous women like Sarah at his beck and call fall for a simple and naive woman like her? History was repeating itself with her like her mother and Kevin O'Connor's disastrous love story.

It wasn't meant to be Ann. It was too good to be true. She thought to herself.

Ann had realized her spiritual upbringing that on this earth nothing here is forever. Phil Jones came into her life suddenly out of the blue and proved her point. *Nothing here is forever.* With that thought, she switched off her cell.

Phil reached home and found Ann missing and her cell was switched off. He confronted Sarah in her room who looked at him innocently with moist eyes, "Phil, she said to me she is leaving because she felt you were putting pressure on her to be intimate with you. She has been through a rough patch in the past and couldn't possibly give herself to a man completely because of her genophobia problem, be it her husband. She will file for a divorce soon she said because she can never be the woman you want her to be."

Phil was devastated. Yet he looked at Sarah suspiciously. She suddenly changed her concerned expression to a more sensuous one. "Phil, I made a mistake. I lost a gem like you. I should never have...I am so sorry. Can't you forgive me? And we start over again once she div..."

Before she could complete her sentence Phil just grabbed her throat in anger and said, "What have you done to her? Did you tell her anything to make her mad enough to leave without meeting or confronting me? I know what you are capable of Sarah. So, blurt it out before I kill you to do so." He thundered in anger. Sarah choked a bit before he left her throat.

"I... you...you blind fool. You reject me for that bundle of nerves. That plain Jane. How dare you. Please leave me alone... I will be gone before you know it in the morning."

Phil gave a disgusted look and left her bedroom. He couldn't imagine what could happen to Ann on the way with the unseen forces closing in on her determined to make their ultimate sacrifice happen at her expense. He needed to move fast. He got into his SUV and left immediately. What Sarah must have told her for her to leave in such a hurry he couldn't fathom. At least Ann should have given him that much credit to wait for him to explain himself.

He had seen the car rental name on the cab that left and knew Mr. Wright, the boss of the services which provided them. He called up Mr. Wright and asked for his help to get him the number of the driver taking Mrs. Ananya Jones or Ms. Ananya Gomez whichever name she gave them to California right now. He was told to wait for ten minutes before the man called back. Phil got the number and name from him and called the driver while he kept driving himself.

"Hello." He heard the man speak on the other end.

"Hi Mr. Green, I am Phillip Jones from the Jones ranch. That's my wife who is traveling with you, Ananya Jones. I want you to slow down so I can catch up with you because she has had a tiff with me and won't speak to me on her cell too. Kindly do this favor so I can make up with her. I just spoke to your boss Mr. Wright who is a friend, and he gave me your number."

The driver knew the Jones brothers because they were socially very popular out there and he was also familiar with their Jones restaurant too as a famous tourist stop. He immediately understood the situation as he looked at a lost and forlorn Ann through the mirror and he said quietly, "Yes sure. Well, I am around ten miles on the way right now. I think I will stop over for coffee at a joint about five miles from here." As he said this, he slowed down his driving.

Ann heard him talk and wondered who he was giving such information to? She got a bit suspicious and was alert suddenly. But the next moment after hanging up the driver said casually to her, "My boss trying to gauge at what time I will reach California. Because he has one more traveler from there tomorrow for Nevada. Thinks I am a machine."

Ann relaxed. So, it was his boss, not Phil. She was relieved though she knew Phil wouldn't stop without pursuing her for whatever his evil plans were. Unless of course, the lust for Sarah got the better of him. That thought hurt and how.

Ann had fallen asleep again thankfully in a dreamless slumber. She couldn't handle a nightmare right now. When she woke up the car was parked in a parking lot of a food joint. There were a few cars parked there and she could see the driver smoking a cigar outside on the porch of the western-styled joint. He must have not wanted to disturb her, so he didn't wake her up. But when she saw the time, it was hardly an hour since they left Phil's house. Why was he taking a break so soon? If Phil was following her, he could catch up with them.

She tried signaling him to move by waving her hands. But he just wouldn't look her way. She finally decided to get off the car and ask him to move fast. Unknown to her somebody was watching her from behind the thicket of tall bushes and shrubs nearby. She walked up to the driver and asked, "Can we move it fast, please. I need to reach my home by dawn."

The driver looked around and said, "Well missus the car is giving trouble that's why I haven't moved yet. Some mechanical issues. Called for another one for you. Waiting."

The fact was he had spoken to Phil who had assured him that he will pay him for the full way. He needn't worry. Phil said he would be there any moment.

Ann exclaimed irritably, "All bad things for me to happen in one day. Aargh...okay, I will use the toilet in the meantime."

The driver pointed it to her as being out at the end of the porch. She went towards it stomping away in frustration. As she was about to open the door of the toilet, she heard a shuffle of footsteps in the bushes just next to the end of the porch near the toilet. Her heart skipped a beat. She couldn't bring herself to open the toilet door. As she tried to move away, she felt someone tug the end of the t-shirt she was wearing under her jacket to stop her. She wanted to scream but her voice was stuck in her throat. It just wouldn't come out. She felt her heart sink as the person holding her there suddenly spoke up from behind and she knew who it was, "Ann don't resist your destiny. You can't run away, baby. That Phil can't save you. He too will be finished if he tries to."

Ann was disgusted and tired of being scared and running away all the time. She needed to stand up to this and face the fear now. She took a deep breath and as she was about to turn behind to look, she heard a loud voice call out her name. It was Phil from the other end of the porch opposite to her. She looked in despair. Did trouble have to come from all sides? The grip on her t-shirt was suddenly let loose. Now she turned behind and there was no one there. She felt anger replace her fear as she turned back and saw Phil approach her.

"Stay away from me. I have nothing to say to you. Just stay away."

She cried out as she held her hands to keep him as far off from herself. Phil walked defiantly towards her and she felt scared as she remembered what Sarah had said about him getting violent and also that he would hypnotize her to do what he wants. She could see his eyes changing color to blue in anger. She avoided direct eye contact with him. He reached her in a few strides and took hold of her arms tightly. He was quite angry because he was hurting her arm.

"The audacity of the man. She should be the only one fuming right now," she thought.

"What do you think you were doing? Who do you think you are to walk out like that on me? Without a slight explanation as to what happened?" He asked with a tone full of hurt.

"Leave me alone. I don't want to create a scene here. You come to California tomorrow and we will talk in my house there," she said with an assertiveness that made her feel stronger.

Phil said, "You are not going anywhere, Mrs. Ananya Jones. Not without me. You want to go to California. We will go together tomorrow. Right now, you are coming with me."

He pulled her arms a bit stronger as she resisted. There were people near the food joint chatting outside, mostly revelers. So, Ann stopped resisting and walked along with Phil quietly as to not draw unnecessary attention. But she didn't want to go with this mystery man she didn't recognize anymore.

She saw the driver of her cab standing there grinning at Phil. So, it was all planned. She should have known. As he approached Phil, he gave him the amount decided for the trip.

Ann looked at the driver and said, "I will complain about you to your boss whoever it is. I will sue your company you wait and watch."

The driver waved goodbye and moved towards his vehicle grinning all the way.

She is really angry, Phil thought. Whatever made her change her behavior towards him so drastically, he had to find out. Though he already knew, it was Sarah for sure.

He forced her to sit in the seat beside him. He started the vehicle and moved. Ann was scared of him. She needed to call for help. She had Matt Johnson's number, but it was eight hours drive from there. At least he could call the police in this area and inform them to help her. She could also take a flight to John Wayne Airport (SNA). But she didn't know these parts in Carson that well. She needed to act cleverly.

She didn't want to scare her parents on the phone. So, Matt would be the right guy. Because knowing Phil, he must have a good rapport with the cops in his area as he had a good civilian facade around him. *Just like Kevin O'Connor*, she thought. So, she decided not to resist Phil and once they reach his place, she will excuse herself to the bathroom and then call Matt. He would surely ridicule her stupidity of trusting Phil Jones, but she could live with that.

Chapter 18

Phil didn't ask anything on the way. He looked hurt and kept silent. But he didn't go back to his place, instead, he drove into Carson City's downtown and checked into a luxury hotel owned by one of his close friends as she heard him speak on the phone. He took a suite room there. Ann was intrigued and scared as to what was he up to. She didn't want to find out, because she would call Matt soon and he would get her the help from the authorities.

As she followed him without resistance, he looked at her without taking his eyes off her. They were shown their beautiful cottage suite. Once Phil shut the door Ann was about to excuse herself to the bathroom when he suddenly held her towards the wall behind her. She couldn't move with the pressure of his body pressed against hers. She decided she wouldn't turn weak now. She looked at him defiantly in the eye to resist him.

He asked her with indignation, "What is it, Ann? Will you tell me, or should I tell you? What did Sarah say to you to make you so mad at me? That you were leaving me and going away? You also told her, of all people, that you couldn't be the woman I wanted you to be and that you are soon filing for a divorce? Why her, Ann? Why not say all that to me?"

Ann looked shocked suddenly. She never said that to Sarah. Something dawned on her suddenly and she asked Phil, "Did you also tell her about my stepfather Kevin's secret dark cult and my phobia problem?"

Phil was shocked as he began to understand some things himself. "No. Never. What did she tell you, Ann? For heaven's sake blurt it out." Phil asked impatiently. Ann then told him everything that Sarah had revealed to her about him and also his feelings for her and what he would do to Ann once she confronts him about it all.

Phil sat down on the couch with his head in his hand. He suddenly blasted at Ann, "You foolish woman, can't you see?! She has been set up by your stepfather Kevin O'Connor and his secret cult, which she is still a part of. It was she who introduced me to this cult five years back when we had started dating. I kind of took to their ideologies on the surface level because I was an atheist myself back then. But when I reached the inner level of the drugs and sexual orgies involving even minor girls and boys, I resisted and wanted to opt-out. And I did just that, which they didn't take lightly.

Once a part of them you cannot exit when you know their secrets. But I did and I also forced Sarah to leave them. Then we got married. Sarah left the cult but the cult in Sarah didn't leave her because she enjoyed what it offered her. Sensuality, youth, and power. And she was secretly back with them and did all that she could to appease their demonic god, like bringing adultery into our marriage. But that was just the tip of the iceberg I got to know. Then I divorced her. But they got to my Jade through Sarah. They set up some junkies to lure Jade into drugs and then a bad relationship with one of them. She followed him to Los Angeles. The rest you know. But what you don't know is the drug nexus and the flesh trade including some of the missing girls in your area, all are connected to this cult in some way and Kevin O'Connor is now high ranking amongst them.

He had also been running a big undercover drug business even though he was in prison. He was completely an occult master and created all the hallucinations and apparitions to lead you to fulfill what the cult wanted. Even those writings on the ground up in the cottage on the hills were a part of it to bind you up. And now... your human sacrifice is the ultimate appeasement they want to offer as they had initiated you in the past for the same."

Ann just couldn't take it anymore. "Wait...just wait. All this you are telling me now. Why? Why did you hide it all this while from me? When you knew my life is in danger. You kept saving me knowing it all the while who was behind this?" Ann almost shouted.

"I wanted to tell you Ann, but I was afraid you would misunderstand me. And then I wouldn't be able to fulfill my mission. That is to save you from them and also give them back for what they did to Jade. And the only way to do that was to marry you and consummate our marriage. That is the only way to break and thwart the plans Kevin has for you. Because when your husband becomes your head covering of authority you will be set free from the demonic powers and the power held over you."

Ann was taking each word and trying to make sense of it all. She had read it somewhere in the Bible about the head covering of authority over a woman by her father and then after marriage the husband to resist the fallen angels.

"But how can Kevin O'Connor? He is still in prison. And how come you are not harmed, and they don't do things to you?" Ann still wasn't sure. Her trust was shaken.

Phil sighed. This had to be done someday. Better it is all off his chest right away. "Kevin was out a year back. I too got know recently when I did some investigation after you said you saw him in dreams and apparitions. Then I saw him too, that night in the woods. But I know they are using all kinds of occult techniques on your mind, playing on your fears to get you. I feel that all these years of your phobia problem was orchestrated by them in your life. So that you never get married to anyone. Since I know all their secret practices and rituals in-depth, they couldn't get a strong grasp on me, though they tried. Rather, they are scared of me revealing all about them to the authorities, which I plan too once I have solid proof on hand against them."

Ann felt foolish now and confused too. Should she trust Phil or Sarah? What Phil said fell in place and made sense. But what Sarah said also made sense then. *Who is true? Oh, good Lord help me to decide.* She cried in her heart. As if as an answer to her prayer, Ann got a call from her mother, Elena Gomez. It was midnight. Ann wondered what was wrong as she picked the call, "Ann are you okay? My child, I had a dream just now with you and Phil in it. You were drowning in some dark waters. Then I saw the good Lord send him to help you. You must stay together Ann. I feel he has been sent to help you." Elena took dreams very seriously as a way of God talking to us sometimes. Ann believed that too.

When Ann had reassured Elena that they were very much together and all was fine, she put the phone off and looked at Phil with a pang of guilt that engulfed her soul. He had his back turned to her. He was visibly angry and rightfully so. How does she make it up to him? Just a sorry will not do right now.

Phil turned to her all of a sudden with hurt in his voice as he said, "Okay Ann... I think I can drop you at your parents by morning. Let's leave now as it's a long drive." He looked defeated and sad.

Ann sat down on the bed as she had tears rolling down her cheeks. "Can't you forgive me just this once Phil? I have wronged you by doubting your character and integrity. I know and accept it. But you did give me reasons to misunderstand by hiding so much from me. I should have asked you and clarified things before running away but I did not. I am sorry Phil. I... I was jealous of Sarah and you and that's why I believed whatever crap she said to me."

Phil turned to her and suddenly his expression changed. He picked her up, his anger being replaced with love, as he said very softly wiping her tears, "One crap of hers is true of what she told you, Mrs. Ann Jones. That I can be demanding...very demanding." saying this he took hold of her and started to kiss her. She kissed him back through the fresh tears of joy that flowed now. He picked her tears off her face with his mouth softly. Then a frenzy of desire followed as if there was no time to lose. She was readily giving her whole mind, body, and soul to this man. But he wasn't any man, he was her lawfully wedded husband and she belonged to him as he did to her. Phil said in a heavy voice looking at all of her, "Ann, my mermaid, you are beautiful, my love."

The intensity of their love for each other was so strong and full of pure desire that her mind had stopped thinking right now so that she didn't realize that her breathing was turning erratic as to when she would go in for a panic attack. But suddenly everything seems less important compared to this with him.

He lifted her face to his and she felt a shudder run through her body because his eyes were filled with the myrrh of desire. He kept looking at her holding her gaze as he lifted her in his arms and bought her to the large bed. As she lay there her heart pounding within the walls of her chest threatening to pop out, she first resisted him with her hands against his chest as she suddenly got flashbacks of how Kevin O'Connor had forced himself on her years back. She looked terrified and Phil understood seeing that look on her face. He softly but assertively said with his eyes holding hers.

"Don't Ann. Don't stop me tonight. I need you to just relax and trust me, sweetheart. I won't hurt you. Just flow with me, will you? Please. We are running out of time. This must take place...now."

And in that now there were no more questions to be asked anymore. She relaxed as she felt they belonged to each other in every sense, before God and man. As she relaxed by taking deep breaths, what followed was a volcano of sensations that erupted in her mind and body. No more fear, no erratic heartbeats, no more breathlessness from the panic attacks. All there was to feel in the moment was pure bliss. For Phil, this was a moment of triumph. He felt like a warrior who had just won the victory in a battle against the evil forces.

The next morning Ann got up feeling like she was in seventh heaven. She felt like a woman in every sense and every part of her soul and body. Liberated like a bird, flying free out of the cage of her mind after so many years of the phobia that gloomed over her life. She found herself crying as she was grateful to God for giving her, Phil. This was it! Finally, it was over the battle over her soul and body from her fears within and the external dark forces outside.

Ann didn't find Phil next to her and neither in the hotel room. She saw the time; it was past ten am. Oh, how much she slept and like a child too. A blissful sleep after ages with no dreams or nightmares. *He must in the bathroom*, she thought, and she went over and found no one in there. She thought he must have had some urgent work after all it was ten am already. He will be back soon she told herself and relaxed again on the bed remembering all those moments of their lovemaking that made her blush now.

She could smell his fragrance on the pillow at the side and it made her want to be with him again. So, she decided to call him on his cell phone and hear his reassuring voice. The cell was switched off. Ann didn't like that as it made her feel a bit uneasy. So, she called the reception down and asked them if they knew anything about Mr. Jones leaving. The call was diverted to the manager of the hotel who told her politely, "Ma'am your stay had been paid for and the car is ready to take you to the airport as your flight to Santa Ana is in two hours from now. Mr. Jones had left in a hurry a couple of hours ago and called back with the necessary instructions. Also, his stuff needs to be left in the room for our staff to collect and be delivered to him when he instructs."

"Oh, okay...I... well thank you," Ann said and kept the phone down.

Ann was baffled and scared beyond words. Her heart was pounding within her and she felt dizzy as she opened the messages on her cell phone and there it was his message sent an hour back:

Dear Ann,

I don't wanna hurt you but can't help it. I didn't have the guts to face you or speak to you in the morning. So, I decided to send you a message instead. I realized after last night that it is Sarah that I want to spend my entire life with. I can't get her out of my mind. I tried my best, but even after being with you, it didn't help me get over her. Go back home, Ann. I cannot live without Sarah and that would be an injustice to you. I think you should consider Matt Johnson too. He cares for you. Your divorce papers will reach you soon. I and Sarah have left for an undisclosed destination together. That's why my cell phone will be off for now. Your flight back home has also been arranged so don't worry about that.

Forgive me if you can, I am sorry.
Phillip

Ann sat there for what seemed a lifetime when finally, she got up with the little strength she had and went to the bathroom. She got freshened up without a single drop of tears falling. She packed her bags and asked about the transport to the airport which was already arranged for and left for home. Her home with the Gomez's and the only home that will be hers to call.

She felt like she was in a zombie state during the flight. Living yet there was no sensation of being alive. All her strength had left her body. She had kept looking at the cell phone 'till her flight took off. Maybe, just maybe he would call and tell her it was a bad joke, a prank he played on her and that he too was there on the flight with her. She had once thought while in the hotel that she must go to the house and check on him. But he had told her he was going away with Sarah. And there was no point in pursuing a man who wasn't happy with her.

When she reached her home and was nearing her neighborhood, she didn't know how she would face her parents. What will she tell them happened to her, her marriage that made them so happy for her? Right now, she felt like a used piece of tissue thrown away unwanted. *Oh, was it better that she had no one in her life more than a week from now? Yes.*

How foolish she had been to trust her entire being to a man she met just a week back. It takes a lifetime to know and trust someone. But she was so vulnerable than that she fell for him, his every word and move. But how, how can someone be so sincere, so full of love and turn a volte-face so suddenly? Last night too was out of the world and as a woman she knew for him as well. She needed to talk to him at least once face to face. But he wasn't interested.

Once home Ann decided against telling the Gomezs everything immediately. They were so happy and elated for the newfound life that she had no guts. She just told them, "He has some very urgent work he had to leave out of town for. Will be back and then I will join him." She lied.

She had never lied before to them or anyone and hated herself after saying it. She hated him too. Hated having trusted him. All those moments when he said he felt something while praying to God, believing in Him, so was it all pretense just to get to her? But why? Why in the world her? Then suddenly realization dawned on her. It has to do with that God-forsaken cult that had destroyed her life and the life of so many young girls like her. He did it for them because he must still be a part of them. Aren't they full of filth and deceit?

"I will get to the bottom of this. I will now confront those guys and Kevin O'Connor too if need be." She promised herself.

The days flew by. She dreaded when the divorce papers would arrive, and she would have to tell her parents the whole truth. She laughed at herself and her foolish naivety. How could she have trusted a Las Vegas marriage to last? Idiot.

"I don't deserve to be a counselor anymore as I don't trust my judgments." She battered herself even further.

But then she did join work again and the next few days it was her work that became her solace and like a facade to hide her emotions behind. Then Matt Johnson came to see her at the community center to congratulate her for the Vegas wedding. She was conscious of him staring at her trying to read between the lines. He was a cop after all.

"You don't seem yourself, Ann. Everything alright? I expected a happier Mrs. Ann Jones looking back at me." He asked.

"Yeah... all fine...Matt...I... can I speak with you later....I...," Shucks! She was so vulnerable right now. Why did he have to come at this moment? She turned her face and pretended as if there was something in her eye. Matt came forward and tried removing it knowing she was lying to him. When she suddenly burst out with all the pent-up emotions.

"Leave me, alone will you? What have you come to see whether whatever you warned me about Phil has come true? Yes. It has. Are you happy now? Just go, okay. Go." She was crying now with immense pain in her heart. Thankfully, there was no one in the room except the two of them. Matt felt very bad for her as he awkwardly came to her and took her head into his chest to console her. She didn't resist because she didn't make anything out of it or anything else anymore. She just cried her heart out and Matt let her be. When he left, she was much lighter from the excessive crying. All she managed to tell him was a, "Thank You".

He nodded as he said, "See you later. But let me tell you, Ann. Sometimes there's more than meets the eye."

What did he mean by that in context to her state right now she wondered?

The days turned into a month. The Gomez's had to be told the truth. They were devastated more for their girl than themselves. Ann felt sorry for them. Their desire to see their grandchildren would well remain just that, a desire.

The divorce papers still hadn't come from Phil. Ann thought she will file for it rather. But she felt at least once she should go back to Carson City and confront him. After all, she wasn't his girlfriend but his wife. But then all her courage left her when she read his message again and again. And the fact that he had not called or come for her all these days. His cell phone was permanently disconnected. He must have taken a new number. So much for avoiding her?

But one thing she was sure of and determined to do. She was going to confront the guys who were responsible for all this in her life, including her stepfather Kevin. And with God-given courage, she was very close to finding out where she could locate them with her resources.

Chapter 19

A ray of hope, a warmth of comfort, for the forlorn and cold despite belonging to the cinders.

Learning to love, learning to hope against all odds & overcoming the fear that hinders.

Then it is shattered, and all of the hope lost, burning again the cinders all over.

All the beauty and love are gone, now accept your fate Cinderella, for nothing here is forever....

A drop of tear fell on the diary as Ann left the poetry there... she shut it with a sigh. No call, no communication yet from Phil, and neither the divorce papers. So, she had applied for them sending him a notice across by her lawyer. There was no answer to that too. Matt Johnson had asked her out a couple of times for dinner. But she had politely declined. For one she hadn't got over Phil one bit since then and secondly, she was still legally his wife. She was in no mood to join the likes of Sarah. Her faith in God had grown stronger if anything in these difficult moments.

And we know that in all things God works for the good of those who love him, who have been called according to his purpose. (Romans 8:28)

Yet another of her favorite Bible verses that always came to her when she was down and low.

She was super low these days even physically and couldn't pinpoint what it was until she realized, she had missed her date of chumming. In all her tension she hadn't noticed it. She did a home test that day. And her fear came true. She was pregnant. With Phil's baby! No... not one more challenge to handle right now...But she would have to keep it...there was no question about that as she supported pro-life.

"Ann girl, you have given us the greatest news ever. We are so happy though for you I wish it were under better circumstances." Said Cristian as he hugged and kissed her. Elena was a bit more tensed, her motherly instincts taking over.

"Child, I know you are in a very delicate situation right now. So, if you feel you are not ready for this...you can...you know you are the most important person in this world for us."

Ann hugged her and kissed her with tears in her eyes. "Mom. I am married and this is not a fatherless child. I am ready for this. The innocent one is at no fault anyway. I am keeping it."

Elena smiled through her tears. "Girl, I pray to God that He gives you lasting happiness in this lifetime. Sadly, I will not be of much help when it comes to guiding you through those crucial months." Elena said sadly as she had never gone through a pregnancy.

Ann hugged her and held Cristian's hand and said, "I need both of you to just keep loving and believing in me as always. That's enough."

****

Days flew by into months. It was the third month complete since Phil had left her, and she was now three months pregnant too. And the bump was showing a bit. Apart from occasional dizziness and mild nausea, she was doing fine. The baby was doing well too she was told by her Gynecologist and it was going to be a girl. Ann felt extreme emotions of all kinds these days. Especially when she visited her mother Sujata at the mental health care facility.

She now saw her mother in a different light. She felt she understood her better now and loved her even more than ever. Sujata wasn't doing well again. Hers was a degenerative mental illness apart from the schizophrenia she had. It wouldn't get better unless maybe she was taken to places that bought back good memories. Ann recently was seriously considering going to Sujata's hometown in Kerala, India, and discussed with her adoptive parents her plans. Also, she planned to give birth to her baby there so that she would have a change of atmosphere too.

The Gomez's were surprised at the thought of having the baby born in India. But they were nevertheless supportive. Elena offered to go with them. She would need help with a mentally unstable woman along. But Ann said she would do just fine as there was a facility in Kerala too whom the doctors here had coordinated with. So, she will be taken care of there and Ann would stay at their ancestral home which still had her maternal aunty, a widow living there with her kids. She had been in touch with her over video call and she was excited to have them there.

"You will be needed here mom, with dad. Who will take care of my dada?" Ann reasoned with Elena. She continued, "As soon as the baby is born, I will be back with her and Sue."

So, the preparations began for the necessary documents and visas. Her Gynecologist was okay with her traveling as she and the baby were healthy and as long as she took care of herself while traveling.

The letter sent forward by her lawyer filing for divorce came back unanswered twice, reason being that the recipient wasn't available at the address. She was in wonder as to where Phil had whisked off with Sarah for so long. Was he so lost in his desire for that woman that he forgot he had to send forward the divorce papers himself?

Matt Johnson had come twice during these days since she told him of her pregnancy and her plans to go India. He was very restless as if he had something to say to her but couldn't. So, she finally asked him, "Matt, what is it? I feel you want to say something important to me, but you are not able to. Do you want to? You can, because nothing shocks me anymore."

Matt seemed to mug up courage as he said clearing his throat, "Ann, I can't live in peacekeeping this to me any longer. But please don't misunderstand me. I was told to do this. I already understood we don't have a future together because you are still madly in love with Phil...Phil is in jail Ann, undergoing a trial for the murder of Sarah Smith, his ex-wife."

Ann felt the earth shake beneath her. This was too much to handle even though she had become quite strong in the last few months. She just fell on the couch staring at the wall in the front.

"I am so sorry Ann should have told you earlier. But he wanted you and me to be together when he pretended to take you out of his life in Carson City that day. He was arrested that morning as the police found Sarah's body strangled in his house after an anonymous caller tipped them. The fingerprints on Sarah's neck matched Phil's and the hour too when he had left the house to pursue you. He was called to the house at the crime scene and then taken to the police headquarters there. He didn't want you to be dragged into it all, after all, you have been through and that's why he wrote that message to you, so you carry on with your life. He saw a long haul in the case ahead. All proof was pointing against him though he told me he hasn't done it. He just pressed Sarah's neck out of anger to make her say where you were that night before he left her alive and well at his place. That's the fingerprints they must have got of his on her neck," Matt sincerely said, trying to help her ease her pain.

Ann just kept staring at the wall ahead of her. She remembered Kevin's words when she heard his voice behind her back that night, "Phil....will be finished too." She shuddered remembering it.

"Ann, I don't know Phil that well, but I do know a lot of people from other cases I have dealt with. He is telling the truth. He didn't want you to get entangled in the case, so he sent you away. He hasn't revealed anything about you to the authorities there. And that's why the case stands against him with unanswered questions. He loves you, Ann. More than you can imagine."

Ann felt silent tears flow slowly down her cheeks. She looked at Matt, "You should have told me earlier and spared both of us from all this pain and suffering. I would have been there to help him out of this." She said quietly.

"Ann, he said he was to send you the divorce papers soon. That you would be a free woman to start life afresh. That he could never give you a good future anymore. Maybe I became weak and selfish as you know how I have felt for you almost forever. Then when those papers didn't come probably because he couldn't bring himself to do it and also you didn't respond to me and now your pregnancy, I decided it's high time I to tell you everything going against his wishes."

"Thanks, Matt. I appreciate it." Ann said honestly. "Can you help me with one more important thing? I have the address and the location of a secret cult my stepfather Kevin is involved in. He is out of jail at the moment. I need to meet with him, but I will need you to come with me. They are quite sinister, these people. I have information about them being behind a lot of the drug, flesh trade, and kidnapping cases since the last decade and more so recently. I have been researching through my sources and the internet."

Matt was a little taken aback. Why was she talking about some vague thing that had nothing to do with Phil's case?

"Don't be surprised at me. This has everything to do with my past and Phil's present."

Matt nodded trusting her. "When do you want to do this?" He asked her.

"Tomorrow." She said with a look of determination. There wasn't any time to lose now. She also had her flight scheduled for India end of the next week. She was still angry with Phil. He didn't trust her love enough to share his problem with her.

What kind of marriage is this? Does he even know what it means? Maybe he doesn't see her fit enough to stand by him in the ups and downs of life. So, she would have to make some decisions for the future but only after she met with Kevin O'Connor finally face to face after so many years.

****

Phil was fidgety today feeling restless since morning. He felt as if there was some news to come his way. Some shocking news. The irony of life. He wanted to help Jade to come out from the correctional center soon and here he was in prison awaiting final judgment. He had honestly told his lawyers all there was to be told. They wanted to call Ann for witness as he was with her that night and she had been there at the house too just an hour and a half before the crime. But he refused and asked them to skip that part, which turned everything against him.

Matt had called him in between and told him Ann wouldn't have anything to do with him in that sense. She was still into Phil.

Phil remembered her each moment, each day. He couldn't bring himself to give her the divorce still. But once convicted of the crime, he was going to go in for a long time. He had to do it sooner or later. He would tell his lawyers to do the needful.

Just then he was told he's got a call from Matt Johnson. He went and took it, "Yes Matt. Tell me some good news that she has moved on. It's been a while now." He asked with anticipation.

"Phil...I am so sorry. I had to tell her everything. She is.... well, three months pregnant with your baby girl." Matt told him.

Phil stood still without answering back for a while. Then he slowly asked, "She is keeping it, right?"

"Yes, Phil. Damn it both of you. She loves you still. And no one can change that." Matt said as he hung up.

Phil didn't know how to react. His daughter! Just like Jamie. Someone who wouldn't call him Uncle Phil but Daddy. Now more than ever he wanted to be out and set free from this case in which he was anyways innocent. Now the longing to be with Ann was even stronger as she must need him. Jeff had said they were some loopholes in the case that could work in his favor and also his lawyers told him so. They were trying to work it out. If Ann would have stood witness things would have moved faster.

The next day Ann dressed up extra smartly also carrying her licensed gun along in her purse. She was to meet Matt at the Kevin O'Connor Mansion which had been turned into the main headquarters for the cult activities which they must be doing under the cover of social service under governing organizations, just like a front facade. There were much darker things happening inside that estate, Ann knew out of her past experience.

After several formalities with the security personnel at the gates of the mansion, where her gun was taken away, but Matt was allowed to keep his as he was on duty. She entered in with Matt Johnson, he on his official bike. As they parked their vehicles in the front parking lot of the estate, she realized why she didn't want to come here alone. It made her shaky and jittery all over again as she remembered every single moment spent here in this dungeon of darkness in her childhood.

They reached the front door that was all gothic in style, renovated from what she remembered. The outside structure though well maintained remained the same, a mix of Victorian and gothic style as before. They rang the bell. It was opened by a lady in black formals and again gothic style makeup. She asked about their credentials and whether they have an appointment. Matt showed her his ID and said they needed to meet Mr. O' Connor urgently regarding a case.

"I think you have the wrong name. There's no Mr. O'Connor here. And to meet with anyone here you need a prior appointment and valid papers in hand so...." The lady was cut off with a voice from the other side.

"Let them in Mage. They are my guests...." It was Kevin O' Connor alright but much older, yet fitter than before. Ann froze as he looked at her in the eye and gave her that same sinister grin of his.

Chapter 20

They were seated with Kevin in his rather palatial hall which was renovated to look ultra-mod with a gothic touch to everything visible. It had all the latest gadgets and stuff. As she sat on the super luxurious couch with antique wooden arms, Kevin looked at Matt Johnson and said, "Officer, if you don't mind can I have a word with Mrs. Jones in private?"

Ann was startled. So, he knew of her present status of being married. Knowing that, she felt, he should have no desire for her to be a part of their cult sacrifice as now she had husband's authority over her as Phil had told her. But then, she didn't know what to believe anymore. Matt wanted to resist him, but Ann nodded to him saying it's okay.

Matt went out. He had taken special permission to come here with Ann as he put it across to the seniors relating this case to the investigation of the recent kidnappings and drug scene in their jurisdiction. Officer Harry, his senior, was ok when Matt told him Ann was involved as she had helped solve quite a few of those puzzles in the past.

****

Once Matt went out, Kevin came and sat next to Ann on the same couch. Ann squirmed despite herself. He still bought those dark violent images back to her mind. She wanted to get done with what she was here for and move fast. She hated his presence and he was grinning at her.

"So, should I say you took my words seriously and came back to me but a wee bit too late, baby? You are married to that traitor Phil now. You are, technically, of no use to me in the context I initiated you here and needed you for. 'Till yesterday you only belonged to me, sweet Ann. Me. And through me to his majesty." He said mystically.

Ann was feeling the anger rise in her. His majesty. So that's what they call their evil demon 'god'. To whom they forever sacrifice the future of young children and people's sanity.

"I have come here only for one purpose. My husband Phillip is in jail in Nevada over the murder of Sarah, his ex-wife. I remember what you said. If he helps me, he will be finished too. So, from what I understand, in order to get even with Phil, it is you who got Sarah Smith murdered. She, who was your pawn, was being used to break us up. Right?" She wasn't afraid in that way anymore. She had the strength of her faith and well also the fact that she was now married to Phil Jones by Kevin's confession.

He looked at her sinisterly before he lit a cigarette surely with some substance in it, she thought. He offered her, "I am sure you still take it, Ann. You were quite high on it when I last knew you." He laughed wickedly.

Ann turned her face away with disgust. How can a human fall so low was beyond her comprehension? Sin made man into a monster. *God give me patience*, she prayed silently sitting there.

"Well, you're accusing me is more on emotional grounds than on actual evidence, isn't it? Do you have proof I killed Sarah? Or anyone else?" He asked confidently.

Ann felt anger rise in her all of a sudden maybe pent up inside her all these years. Though she was also nervous at the same time as she had something in mind and hoped it would work. "Well, I am the proof. Your record and who you are is proof enough. Also, the fact that Phil had the guts to stand and give it back to you by saving me and avenging his sister Jade, the two most important women in his life whom you have tried to destroy completely. The fact is he has started believing in God as I do, who is supremely more powerful than all powers put together in the universe, and the 'majesty', as you call him, cannot harm a hair on our heads because of Him."

Kevin laughed sarcastically looking at her and said, "Spiritual fools.... then may I ask how come you are here meeting me? For what purpose?"

Ann was being affected by his eyes looking right at her in a menacing way. She could see those moments spent in this very place years back and they flashed before her eyes. His atrocities on her mother and her. She mugged up all the courage she had to boldly reply, "Only to tell you this, that if you don't clear Phil's record, because he is innocent of Sarah's murder, then there will be consequences to you and this cult of yours..." She managed to say it all without stammering, though she felt she would if she lost control now.

"Haa...haaa...haa…" It was a burst of long laughter that echoed in the tall walls of the living room. Then he was all of a sudden serious and he got up and came and stood before her and he sat down near her knees looking at her face. "Ann, Ann sweets...you are as naive as you were when you were a kid. I had great plans for you. Look at me, I am richer and more powerful than I ever was. In jail all this expanded, for I didn't need to be physically around to make it all happen. Would have kept you like a princess if you had cooperated with us. You gave me in then and you threaten to do so again?" he said now, standing up, thundering.

"You are such a fool, can't you see? I told you Phil will be finished, and he is. There's no way of getting him out of there. No. Because the fingerprints were his on her neck. We didn't even have to send someone across to do the job on Sarah. It was all done from here by powers that are beyond anyone's imagination and gained not by small sacrifices and appeasements. So now I put a proposal before you..." he said, with much pride as he looked at the little swell of Ann's tummy. With vengeance in his eyes, he continued, "Your baby. After 6 months more. You will give her to me. You will stay here with me in this mansion all through your pregnancy. This is the condition to get Phil out of prison and you know I can bloody well do that too."

Ann was flabbergasted. So, he knew of her pregnancy. She knew these people had their eyes everywhere. But what was he implying? Was he out of his mind? She knew what he was planning to do with her baby. Over her dead body, she would give Phil and their baby to this monster. Ann thought to herself as she shuddered. But she knew she had to play her cards well.

"And you will have to leave that God of yours too when you come to me. I will be your only god for as long as you are here." He said smiling diabolically.

So, he was afraid of God and her faith. That gave her renewed strength and also a revelation that this is where they were not able to do much harm to her and Phil. Someone was protecting them all the way. She could see Kevin had predetermined she would do as he says. *Let him think that way*, Ann smiled to herself. She knew what she would do.

"Okay. So, I will do as you tell me. But Phil's release must happen immediately. Then I will come and stay...." She was cut off by him abruptly.

"No, darling. I am not a fool. I am also a businessman if you have forgotten in that cute head of yours. You come and live here first and I get him out immediately after that." He grinned in that unnerving evil way.

Ann swallowed. This was unexpected. But no worries. She had a backup plan in her mind. "Okay... I will come tomorrow evening itself. Is that fine? But if I don't get the news of him being released soon, Matt Johnson will see that I am out of here." She said, now a bit unsure how she will bring herself to be under the same roof as Kevin O'Connor.

Kevin smiled, pleased with himself. Matt was called in who looked at Ann questioning if everything was alright. She assured him with a nod.

When they left from there Matt and she went to the precinct. Once in his office, Matt asked her what had happened with Kevin. She told him everything.

"Are you out of your mind? Did you agree to go and live with this demon? In his place? Why? Ann, Phil will get out sooner or later when he is declared innocent. You don't..." Ann cut him off.

"Matt. Listen to me. I have a plan. And I have already taken the first step to it." She showed him an object that she took out from the front pocket of her jacket. Matt's expression changed. It was a small chip camera in a pen.

A week later Phil was released from prison. Jeff was there to pick him up.

"How did this happen? I am still confused. They are saying they got evidence of some footage that I had left the house minutes before Sarah's death. That is what I have been trying to tell them all the while. The exact time I left the house and the time of her murder doesn't match. Plus, the fact that there was no weapon on the crime scene." Phil told his brother on the way. But still, it was almost unbelievable he got out so quickly just like that.

"Bro. I am sorry. Since Ann has come into your life; I find everything going bad for you. We were so happy before it all. And now even Sarah..." Jeff was very blatant in his tone of not being so fond of Ann.

"Let me correct you. Initially, I came into Ann's life as a plan to get to Jade, as I had told you everything when I left for Orange County. She has been in more trouble because of me. Anyways, let's face it, life has not been the same for us since Jade left. As for Sarah, I never wanted this to happen to her. But she called for it, what with the kind of people she was associated with."

Jeff was silent. Phil was right in a way even though he found the likes of Sarah more of a suitable partner for him. "Now what, bro? Ann and you are...err...kind of separated due to whatever you told her earlier. And now you are telling me she is pregnant with your baby. I think you should sort this out soon before things get more bitter." Jeff said with maturity knowing the importance of a family himself.

"Also, now that you are out, and Jade will be back soon too. The lawyers have appealed for a fresh investigation in her case as she has provided them with some new evidence. Once she is back, I am thinking of going on a long vacation with Rudy and Jamie. She's been longing for quality time together for some time now. You and Ann can together take care of the ranch and restaurant for some time." He smiled.

Phil smiled too. Rudy had told him when she came to visit him once in prison, how Ann had brushed her up on spending quality time with her husband to have a deeper understanding between them. She said they needed to add some romance to their routine life. Well, Ann! So, understanding and mature in many things...how he wished he was already there and holding her in his arms right now. He longed for her so much that it hurt in his heart. And to think of it he had decided no woman would ever do that to him and had stuck to that resolution until he met Ann.

Phil called Ann's number immediately after reaching home. But there was no response. He called Matt Johnson as he packed to leave for California to the Gomez's house. He was determined to get them back as soon as possible, his wife and his baby girl.

Matt sounded a bit low and very discreet when he told Phil over the phone. "Well Phil, I have been waiting to talk to you. But I think it would be better if you come over to California first. Can't be told over the phone."

Phil felt a sudden fear, "Is...is Ann okay...?

"Oh yeah, Phil. Just that she...well...she isn't at home. She has been at the O'Connor mansion for the past week. Why, what, all this I can only explain when you are here."

Phil was furious beyond control as he drove his car way too fast. What the heck was Ann doing in that diabolical place with Kevin O'Connor out from prison? Did he trick her into it or use his occult magic arts over her mind? He would kill someone this time and it would be Kevin O'Connor if he harmed her and his baby in any way.

It was a week since Ann moved into the O'Connor mansion. She got the news that Phil had been set free. Things were moving as planned with Matt and the concerned authorities involved discreetly. She had also managed to get some information that could help in Jade's case and it was passed on to the cops. But Kevin was too cunning, and an old player and she couldn't be presumptuous about him. He could notice things with an eagle's eye and to top it she was now in the lion's den itself. Having said this, she was being treated like a queen with all the nutritious foods provided and luxuries at her beck and call. There was always a doctor ready and a helper maid who looked as sinister as the interiors of the mansion, to attend to her twenty-four/seven. As if Kevin was trying to show her what she might have enjoyed, had she agreed to be one with them willingly. But now Ann shuddered at the thought of him wanting to harm her baby.

Phil will surely try to get in touch with me here. I hope Matt is able to convince him of our plan. Ann thought. She couldn't personally talk to Phil. Not in this place, no. Phil was finally out but now she was at the mercy of Kevin and his cult and they could do anything to her if they found out.

"What's on the mind of my little girl may I ask?" Kevin came towards her from behind.

Thank God they had no access to the thoughts of a person unless of course when in their mind control. Ann looked at him and forcibly smiled, "No, I was just thinking now that Phil is out, and he will try to search for me. If he does find out, please see to it that no harm is caused to him if he comes here for me." Ann said it as it was.

Kevin's old but-toned face darkened. "You love that man way too much...what does love give you people after all? Your God talks of love and you believe Him and then see what happened to your Sue? A hopeless case of love." He laughed.

Ann wanted to slap him hard but controlled her instincts.

"Well, you can, in fact, go back to him if you promise not to disclose what happens here...but that's once we have your baby." He smiled wickedly at the last words. Ann knew he was a liar, so she hardly believed him. They must have already planned a way to get rid of her after her delivery or maybe right at the delivery. It was all so easy for him.

Ann's lips quivered at the possibility of things not going her way. There's always an uncertainty to every plan after all. "Sure...thanks." She said trying to sound as calm as possible.

The next morning Kevin left for some urgent work for a whole day to some undisclosed destination and Ann sort this as an opportunity to get more evidence around the place against him. Her mission was to end this chapter of this cult and Kevin O'Connor once and for all.

Even as a child when she was living here there were places, she wasn't even allowed to explore. And she was too scared of Kevin to do so too. Ann now went for a walk around the property with that spy of a helper not around her as Ann had purposely upset her entire room and messed up her clothes and stuff around, then asked her to get it sorted. That would keep her busy for the next hour at least Ann thought. In the last week, Ann had explored the older building but found nothing suspicious. But Ann noticed that towards the back of the mansion there was an expansion of a new structure that matched the older building which was just single-storied.

She had never seen it here years back. *Must have been built much later*, Ann thought. And behind that beyond the high wire fencing were dense woods as before. She now moved slowly towards the building which was made from the same Victorian styled stones of the older building and the gothic architecture. As she looked around to see no one was watching her she tried opening the heavy wooden door.

"It won't open, damn it...a roadblock again." She said in a whisper. She was talking to Matt about the devices they had given to her according to their plan. It was a small chip kind of device that delivered live footage in real-time and was fitted into her hair two places back and the front. She also had a micro bug device fitted into her ears so she could hear them from the other end and respond too. *Thanks to technology*, Ann thought, a *man was capable of doing such great things as these, as well as so much evil like Kevin.*

She went behind the building to see if there was another way to get in there. Somehow, she felt it held the keys to a lot of the mysteries locked up right now. As she explored behind, she almost felt like Sherlock Holmes, albeit a pregnant one. She smiled at how bold she had become since Phil came into her life. She sighed. How she missed him especially now when danger lurked all around her.

Matt and officer Harry were watching keenly as Ann moved around, on the monitor screen at the police department. Officer Harry spoke up, "Ann. Listen to me carefully. You can abort this mission, Ann. We will look into it with our trained sleuths. We can come to rescue you in an hour. Now that Phil is out. You are putting not only yours but also your unborn baby's life in danger there."

Ann was almost tempted to say yes. But she took hold of her emotions and said quietly, "No Officer. It's me or no one this time. Only I have the access to do this or that door of mystery will shut forever. And then the atrocities will continue for the innocents like I was once. The Claras, Millies, and the Jades will suffer....and no guarantee what he can do to Phil and me and our baby too in the future. And the biggest factor is he is now even more influential with much higher connections we cannot even fathom. Without evidence, you all will not have access to anything of his. But have patience we are closing in on him. I can feel it."

Saying this she moved towards the small glass windows on the lower end of the building. It was an indication there was a basement underneath. But there were too small for her to get in and were tightly shut. And the window glasses were not the see-through ones. There must be some evidence of their crimes hidden inside for sure Ann thought. Then she noticed an insignificant door at the back right at the end of the basement windows, like a back-door type. She suddenly heard some noises of people talking coming from inside the door and she hid quickly behind some tall bushes. There came out a man and a woman with cleaner's aprons on. They looked as stoic as the rest of the staff at O'Connor's mansion.

The man said to the woman, "We'll finally shut it after giving them supper as usual. The bloody lock needs to be changed. It's too difficult to open each time."

The woman nodded. So, he latched the door and put the lock on the handle without actually locking it giving it an illusion of being locked. Then they left.

Ann quickly ran and opened the latch of the door quietly. She heaved a sigh of relief. She kept whispering commentaries on the things around as all this was also being recorded by the concerned department of police via the bugs. "Wonder who they are going to give supper to inside here," Ann whispered through the device to Matt.

She hardly had forty-five minutes before her helper would come looking for her. She moved inside slowly as it was dark, and a sickly damp smell hit her nose. It bought back memories of the initial places Kevin would take her and her mother for the rituals before this house became their favorite ceremonial center.

Ann saw after a few steps that there was a two-door entrance to what seemed like a huge hall on the upper floor. She peeped in and it looked like a place for administrative work and community gatherings with a library of books all around on the walls. *Surely a facade to mislead the law*, Ann thought. She was anyways more interested in the spiral of stone steps going down probably in the basement of the building. It was dark on the steps and she had no torch nothing whatsoever with her.

Kevin had taken away her mobile phone and she was made to speak to her parents only twice a week in his presence. The Gomez's had been told by her that she was on an official mission trip with Matt and Officer Harry too and would be back in a week. Matt had assured them too. If she had revealed she was going to the O'Connor mansion Cristian would never have let her.

As Ann moved down carefully putting her feet on the first step and then the second holding onto the wall on the side, she was shocked because as she moved there were dim lamps that lit up on the way automatically. Quite advanced for a place like this. She could hear Matt telling her to be careful down there.

There was a labyrinth of corridors in the basement. She went to the main corridor and saw there was nothing much there as evidence except for strange-looking empty rooms with just some vocational training equipment in each. She tried one after the other, but every room had stuff in there that made no sense for what she was looking for. Ann found it useless to explore here but Matt and Harry kept telling her it was all-important for them to record.

As she moved into the fourth corridor, she felt something below her feet like a hollow sound that felt different from a little ahead of it and a little behind. There was a carpet on the floor all over. She remembered she had a knife in the shape of a pen for safety in her secret jacket pocket. That was a thumb rule with her. She took it out and ripped the carpet with a little struggle, but the knife was sharp enough.

Below the ripped carpet was a wooden door. She tried opening it with great effort and it still wouldn't budge. There wasn't even a visible lock system to it. Then Matt guided her to look out for a lever or a switch or something that opens it. As she searched all places especially the walls around the door, she found a round button on the wall as she slides her hands on it which was camouflaged to look like a part of the wall itself. She pressed it and the door opened without a sound. She quickly opened it upwards and was shocked to see again there was a spiral of steps going downwards. That meant yet another basement below the first one. Now things were getting interesting and also that much scarier.

Chapter 21

The stairway down was dark but thankfully had sensor lights and, on each step, as she took them the dim lights lit up. Ann's heart began to pound. From experience, she knew these places carried an air of diabolical energy and demonic presence as these people blatantly worshiped the devil as their god. She almost felt like she was in Hell. She kept remembering God all this while. All the faith she had developed in these years with the Gomez's came and stood like a pillar of strength within her soul. She had prayed before venturing out on this mission and had been doing so regularly since the last one week but in the secret as one of Kevin's conditions was not to mention God there.

As she moved stealthily down the steps that seemed never-ending as this basement must be at least three floors down Ann calculated, toward its end again there was a long single corridor which was in pitch darkness now as there was no way of light to enter there. And strangely the auto lights didn't light up here. What was wrong?

"Damn," she said to herself. She had just half an hour before that helper lady would look out for her and one last week left before flying to India with Sue. She had to find something against Kevin that would ensure the closure to him and his evil cult.

She was disappointed and decided to come some other time with a torch maybe as there was no way of going into the pitch darkness. Who's to know what may be there. Officer Harry and Matt also advised her against it. So, she turned to go back and come tomorrow with a torch. When suddenly she heard something move near the stairway on top. His heart missed a beat. She quickly took advantage of the darkness down and slowly with the help of the stone walls kept moving in. By the end, the wall bent towards the right she could feel but not see and she hid around the turn and waited. Matt and Harry were tensed on the other end as they couldn't see a thing and told her to be silent and careful.

Ann could hear something moving in the dark towards the corridor end. She felt her heart pounding so loud that maybe it would start to echo in that corridor and give her up she thought. She closed her eyes as she prayed silently. Then she began to catch the wall and move even further towards the other end. As she moved swiftly without a sound, she hit against a dead-end wall with nowhere to go further as she felt the walls with her hand. She slid herself towards the other side of the corridor and yet there was nothing there. No door, no passage leading to any other corridor. Just plain stone walls she could feel with her hands. The sound of someone moving in the corridor got closer. Suddenly her heart sank. This was it? Her end with whatever was there in the dark coming towards her?

Ann silently listened to the sound of the movement approaching towards her trying not to breathe too loud. She couldn't give up without a fight she thought. Enough of the fear and being scared of it all her life. She thought she would make a dash for safety as a last chance at least and would run in the dark towards the steps of the corridor where the sensor lights would light up. So, she took a deep breath and ran for her life but before she could take a turn at the corridor she was caught by strong hands against the wall and a palm put on her mouth to stop her from shouting. She felt petrified and trying to adjust in dark to see who that figure was before her. She didn't need to see any further because she felt his warm hand on her mouth and smelt his fragrance and knew it was Phil. He took off his hand from her mouth as she relaxed. She said breathing hard and, in a voice, choked with emotion, "Phil... it's you." Was she relieved to have him here? But it wasn't safe for him to be here.

She opened her mouth to say something but before she could he just pushed her hands to the wall behind and kissed her, but there was a violent anger Ann felt in it, so much so that she whimpered in pain. She struggled to move away. When he moved his mouth off hers, he thundered in anger close to her face, "How dare you come here and even think of such a deal with that monster? Even if it's a plan as Matt told me. How can you, Ann? How can you put your life and our baby's life in danger? How?" He sounded very angry as she couldn't see his face clearly but only the silhouette of his features as her eyes adjusted to the dark. Nor could he see that tears flowed down her cheeks to see him like that. So, the fatherly instincts were making him behave so crazy as to not understand the fact that he wouldn't be out right now if this plan hadn't been put into action. She suddenly felt indignant towards him that after all these months he should only think selfishly for his baby and not understand her stance.

"Let me go, I don't want to talk about it right now as you are not yourself. You go from here. We will talk later when you cool down. Anyway, it's dangerous for both of us to be here together." Saying this she tried freeing herself from his grip as he held her even more tightly and his face was as close to her as possible.

"Don't try my patience, Ann. You are leaving with me right now. And there's no two ways about that." He was about to take her with him towards the steps when he stopped.

Suddenly they could hear a commotion in the upper basement. That meant surely someone found out there has been a breach. Ann said, "Quickly let's see where we can hide fast. Or else everything will be over in vain."

Matt was worried and so was Officer Harry. They could hear Phil had reached there to her and that was a relief, but the noises meant they were both in trouble. Actually, it was Matt who had guided Phil to reach where she was by giving him instructions on his mobile Bluetooth.

Phil remembered and put the torchlight of his cell phone on. Now they could see the dungeon-like corridor clearly and each other too. Phil was still angry with her as he refused to look at her directly. Ann too had her ego, so she didn't confront him. Right now, it was important to find a place to hide. But there was none. Weirdly that was the dead-end of the plain corridor that actually had no doors, no windows nothing at all. *Weird*, thought Phil. Once he had been involved in such places back in Nevada, but each place had its secrets he thought.

"I think there has to be a secret lever or button somewhere which opens to a passage or something behind these walls like the door on the upper basement floor," Ann said more to herself. Phil was a bit amused. She looked like a cop more than a counselor now. How many colors were there for Ann?

Ann looked around in the low light of the mobile. From above, the commotion was growing louder. The helper lady must have finished the work assigned to her and found Ann gone for long and created a ruckus. So, they must be looking for her and must have found the unlocked back door.

As she was lost in her thoughts Phil was exploring the walls when he suddenly alerted her as he touched the walls at the far end of the other side. That was no wall but a large special kind of mirror covering one full side of the wall. The mirror was of unique glass, thought Phil as it could create a foolproof illusion with the reflection from the other wall as if there was a wall there too but because there was no light there he could see himself and Ann in it. He further explored and found there was a narrow passage behind the mirror on both sides and they went behind into the passage. In the end, the passage opened into a wide and tall corridor which lit up with the dim auto lights as they moved towards its end where they found a tall gothic style double door that was shut without a lock.

They opened it slowly without making a noise. There was a very big hall inside where there were dim lights already on, but no one seemed to be there. It was darkish and scary and was a giant round ballroom kind of a place with tall gothic-styled pillars and a high ceiling with a huge dome-like structure that had murals of all kinds of demonic beings and fallen angels depicted in them. That explained why the spiral steps to this basement were at least three floors down.

Although the place smelt of dampness, there was no suffocation as Phil realized despite it being so much below surface level, they must have used some latest technology in the building that even three stories down there was enough oxygen. They shut the large door behind. Then they saw there in the center of the floor around the circle of a weird drawing made of marble, granite, and other mosaic tiles for their ritualistic ceremonies.

A slight elevation and steps were leading to a royal kind of throne. *Must be Kevin's*, Ann thought with disgust. He thought he was a god. Then there were large paintings of naked men and women on the walls, some depicting unspeakable things. But what interested Phil was the one with naked Adam and Eve and the serpent coiled near Eve's feet. He looked at Ann because he knew the story in the Bible about the original sin in the garden of Eden. Ann had suddenly turned pale-looking around. She looked as if she was having a panic attack right there. He worriedly asked, "What happened Ann. Are you ok?"

"This ...is ...exactly ...the replica of ...of...that place where I was ...taken as ...as..." She was crying as she caught Phil's jacket and pushed her face inside it. Phil calmed her by stroking her head and holding her tightly as he clenched his jaws in anger.

Officer Harry and some other authorities who had joined in were now excited as there was some lead they had got here. Matt on the other hand was worried for Ann and Phil. Time was closing in. They had to move fast or hide at least. More evidence was needed than this to corner Kevin.

As they turned to look around the big round hall Ann went closer to all things so that the device could capture all the things possible. *Kevin and his associates shouldn't be let out of prison for the rest of their lives on earth*, she thought. Ann noticed a long closet near one side of the wall. She needed to check that too. As she opened it, she felt dizzy. In were all sizes of black and red robes with hoods and weird masks hanging at the side. She shut it immediately after Matt and all got a good view of it. It reminded her of all her nightmares and hallucination kind of apparitions a few months back.

Phil then saw an altar before the image of a very ugly being at the extreme left of where they stood in the round hall. Ann saw it too, "It's their demon god they call 'majesty' ...I don't remember everything about the place they would take me to very clearly because I used to be drugged..." She said with indignation.

Phil knew much more than her. After all, when he had reached this stage of being a part of this cult, years back, he left the cult because he realized this goriness is not what he had set out for. Their great ideologies that had first impressed him were but just a surface level thing. There were layers underneath to cross before one realizes they are stuck in something so mucky and sinister.

The voices outside were louder now. Phil quickly held Ann's hand and rushed behind one of the many single doors near them in the round hall and shut it behind. They entered into yet another broad corridor with again no lights coming on automatically. Phil wondered why some parts were made without the auto lights in this hell of a place. Then he put on his cell torch, which was quite bright. Phil and Ann were shocked to see that there were secret prison cells in a line in a long corridor again. There were at least twenty on both sides of the long corridor. Ann and Phil walked past each of those cells with the torchlight aimed at them so that Matt and officer Harry could have a decent view of it all.

They couldn't believe their eyes. They were goats in one, sheep in another, all alive but still. As if in a pause mode. Then a couple of the cells were empty. But as they walked further, they saw human beings in the other cells. Mostly young women, one in each cell. And then what they saw shook Ann badly. They saw some younger girls and even boys, kept in a couple of the cells. The strange thing was none of these people were reacting to their presence. As if they had been hypnotized or drugged or both. Then mugging up courage, Ann walked further with Phil's mobile torchlight. She wanted the cops to have a good view of their recording. This evidence was enough for the undoing of Kevin O'Connor, forever

Matt Johnson and Officer Harry had already coordinated with concerned authorities and FBI to reach the place and make the arrests and start the rescue operations. The shady O'Conner estate was already on the radar of the local authorities after Kevin's release from prison. He had very high connections and to date, they couldn't gain access to this.

Ann walked more like a zombie her self-looking at each cell with some young girl ruthlessly taken away from her family and even the few young boys too. Tears streamed down Ann's cheeks as she felt their misery here. Then she was shaken up to see Clara Smith, the kidnapped teenager in one of the cells further, sitting down there with that same lost expression. Ann caught the bars of her cell and called out loud enough so that Clara could listen. "Clara...Clara...it's me Ann. Ananya Gomez. See..." There was a slight shift of her eyes towards Ann. Then she looked away again into oblivion.

Ann began to cry as she held against Phil who let her be there till she stopped. If only he could get hold of the monster Kevin for destroying so many innocent lives. Soon as he thought this to himself there was a loud voice from behind in the dark as someone clapped their hands and the sound sensor lights came on in the entire corridor. It was Kevin looking at them with a wicked grin, "Amazing... what a union. Only it shouldn't have been here in my secret chambers and not before the baby is born."

With him were a couple of his very close associates and a couple of tall henchmen all dressed in black clothes.

"Ann sweets, I thought we had a deal. Surprisingly, you are being who you are didn't keep up to it, but I had more integrity than you. I kept my word with getting Phil out of prison and right next to you. See. But now a breach is a breach. You thought I don't have this place closely monitored? Right on my iPad, I saw the whole drama. I have always had my eye on you. Even when I was in prison, I would keep an eye on you making sure you never got close to anyone. All the while I could see visions during our rituals of a hazy picture of a guy coming to your rescue in the future. With time the picture became clear. It was Phillip Jones of course. I got him to us using the gorgeous Sarah who was an integral part of us. But he seemed to resist most of the things and eventually retracted." He said now taking his attention to Phil from Ann.

"And you Phil, I think you too failed to keep your commitment to us just like Ann. You had promised Ann will be handed over to us by you on the way to Nevada if we released that girl kidnapped that night near the pub, but you went ahead instead and got married to her in Vegas? You two are not trustworthy at all. Moreover, you have seen too much, both of you. Phil of course I have no use of you anymore so you will be disposed of immediately." Kevin said confidently of what he wanted.

Ann just gasped and wanted to retaliate when Phil stopped her. He gave her a look that said play along. Kevin moved a few steps and said, "You, my dear Ann, will give birth to the baby who will be precious to us. We will make sure she is taken *good* care of." He said the last word emphasizing strongly on the good. It sent a chill through Ann's spine.

"And after that, you shall also be suitably discarded." He smiled looking at Ann like a man without a soul. And that was what he was because his soul was already 'sold' out, Ann knew.

Phil who was clenching his jaws and fists with great difficulty controlled his urge to smash Kevin's face up at the mention of Ann and the baby. But he realized it would make all their efforts fall flat. They had to keep Kevin engrossed 'till the authorities reached there. But Kevin was in no mood to be engrossed. He roared like a wild animal in wrath now, "Take him and get rid of this man immediately. As for you, Ann dear. You will stay in the confines of one of these cells for the rest of your term. No moving around, no contact with the world outside. and no freedom. That's the punishment for people who betray me."

As he finished, the two tall and muscular henchmen at his side came to get hold of Phil to take him and go. But Phil had the gun out of his pocket by then. He pointed it to Kevin's henchmen, who still kept walking towards him like robots who were programmed to obey. Phil fired a round each on both their legs. They stopped and fell with pain but still, they looked at Phil and kept crawling towards him.

In the meantime, Kevin also had his gun out which he pointed at Phil's heart, as he smiled and said, "Goodbye traitor. See you on the other side." And he fired a round at Phil but Ann who was there by his side, jumped at once before the bullet could hit him and took it on herself. It hit her in the center of her chest as blood oozed out uncontrollably. Kevin's gun fell in shock from the unexpected turn of events.

Chapter 22

Matt Johnson had heard the commotion through the bug on Ann and knew Ann was hurt as he had heard Phil shout her name in alarm. The recording continued at the station while Officer Harry and others took over there. The concerned authorities and Matt himself was on the way with other officers much before anything had happened there.

Phil had caught Ann in his arms before she fell to the ground. Kevin was stunned. He didn't move immediately. But as Phil couldn't think straight and, in his desperation, he started to call out to Matt about the secret microchip bug on Ann.

"Matt, please call the ambulance to the mansion quick. Ann has been shot by Kevin. Be quick. please." He pleaded.

Kevin realized his actions, his words, and his whereabouts everything was being watched and recorded by the police. "It's a bloody set-up!" He screamed to his equally shocked associates. He picked up the gun with a mad vengeance to shoot Phil this time saying, "Ruination, that's what you both are for me. Especially you Ann, every time I brought you into my life. Both of you and your baby die now."

He prepared to pull the trigger at Phil even as Ann was struggling to stay alive already when the sound of a gunshot went off and yet another. Kevin O'Connor fell on his knees and then face down. It was officer Matt Johnson who had shot him and behind him were other officers and concerned authorities. Also, the paramedics came in and the medical staff with stretchers that took Ann to the ambulance on it and later others from the cells, including Clara Smith. The entire place was ransacked in the investigations and all the arrests made subsequently. Other influential people connected with the cult were to be located and arrested soon with the fresh evidence.

Ann was rushed to the emergency ward of the city square hospital. For Phil, all questions being asked as to what, where, and why just seemed to drift above his head. He kept answering without actually being involved. He was totally lost.

"Oh, why Ann, God why? She is the most important person for me on the earth and now there's our baby too. Please let her be. Let her be. Ann, stay put, sweetheart. ..." He prayed.

It was well past midnight. The doctor had told him it is a complicated case. Though the bullet escaped her heart it has nevertheless resulted in great loss of blood and also some damage to the vital parts around the chest area. The baby too would need special attention due to the trauma of the loss of blood and dehydration caused to the mother.

The Gomez's were inconsolable, especially Elena. They left after visiting hours were over only when Phil said he was there, and he assured them. Nurse Lara came and sat next to him in the waiting area as he refused to budge from there.

"Son ...didn't I tell ya...She is a prize catch. Now I know marriages are made in heaven yeah. You both complement one anotha'. You have always saved her in the nick of time she would tell me. Paid ya debt in a shot this gal, didn't she?" She had moist eyes as she said this.

Phil cried. He had before at Jade's but not like this since adolescence when his mother left them and later when Maria broke his heart as a kid. Right now, he just couldn't help it. Lara was so right about Ann. She was surely a prize catch for him. Now he realized what love at first sight meant when he met Ann but a little late. Now when she was battling for life inside, all his ideologies and his perceived notions about women and how to relate to them seemed so contrived. The very things he despised in youngsters he felt with all his soul. Well maybe because he had never met someone who could have retained so much of the childlike innocence in her soul despite the evil that happened to her. It could have made anyone bitter. But not Ann.

"Don' lose courage...pray mah, son, pray." Lara consoled him. And that he did until dawn.

The next day Officer Harry and Matt Johnson were there at the hospital thankful to Phil and Ann for busting the dark nexus of occult, abductions, and drugs. A lot of arrests were underway in connection to Kevin O'Connor's secret cult and shady networks. The kidnapped youngsters would return to their families once their necessary tests were conducted and counseling therapies were done for them. They had also got enough evidence thanks to Ann, to get Jade out of prison soon too. And officer Harry said Matt Johnson would be going in for promotion. But they couldn't celebrate now. No, not until Ann was out and well.

That morning Ann lay on the hospital bed of the ICCU section where she was on life support after the operation and still battling for life as per the doctors. The whole night she wasn't aware of anything being heavily sedated but now she could sense the room around her. She could see the doctors and the nurses discuss something over her, Nurse Lara too was there looking tense and tired. Then she saw Phil come in and he was looking so not himself with an overgrown stubble and a crestfallen expression.

Why weren't they talking to her when she was looking at them? That's when reality hit her. She was in a comatose state. Breathing but not responding mentally or physically to the outside world. Yet she was so conscious of her being alive still, but then for how long? After all, she was ready for this, wasn't she? Whenever she connected with God on a spiritual level, she was always aware that things here are temporary no matter how wonderful. Everything comes to an end here on earth. Just one thing remains, love. Because it so from God and its essence is eternal. God is Love. With these thoughts she suddenly felt herself being lifted in the air, floating above the hospital room, the roof of the hospital, the sky, and clouds above and beyond the earth itself into a realm of total darkness.

There were two beings at her side full of bright light throughout as if guiding her. She understood they were angels. So, she was dead, is it? She stood not inside the thick ugly darkness but outside it and yet could feel the horrors inside. *This is Hell. But why am I seeing this?* She didn't have to speak it out. The celestial beings at her side spoke inside her mind with no physical words needed.

"So, you can see what you have escaped. And what Kevin O'Connor hasn't."

She saw him almost immediately. He was being tortured and torn apart in his spirit beyond human comprehension. It couldn't be explained in words. But it was so intense the suffering there that Ann felt sad and sorry for him now.

Then she was transported by the beings to a passage full of light and at the end, she stood at the feet of a being whose cool and bright light was different. More powerful than a hundred suns but yet not blinding. She couldn't see Him but heard His voice in her mind again.

"Ann... Ann. My child? You still have unfinished work down there and lots to heal still. I want you to overcome all your fears in your soul. I

will help you so that one day when I will call you back to me you will be ready. Go...go back to your husband and the baby that will be born to you. Bring her up to be fearless in faith. For all that you have been through and endured and for your faith, you will be rewarded. Though nothing is permanent there for you now the good things will last your lifetime."

With this Ann suddenly felt a thrust of energy go through her body and she woke up from the coma at once. She was back. She realized that outside the body there was no concept of time or travel. And she knew in her spirit that it wasn't a dream. It was a real encounter with Him that she had only read and heard of. Now she had seen it herself. She must tell Phil about it too. Phil. She suddenly looked around for him.

He was sitting by her bedside holding her hands and was lost. When she jerked her hands, he looked up and saw her eyes were open and looking at him. He had tears of joy brim in his eyes as he kissed her hand and was about to call the doctor as she stopped him pulling at his hand.

He sat down next to her and said very softly, "Ann darling...sweetheart...Oh, thank God you are okay, darling...I promise you I will never hurt you again my love. I will never leave you and let you out of my sight. Thank you, Lord... Now do I believe with all my heart He exists. He does. And thank you Ann for so many things," he said putting his hand on her tummy.

Ann smiled at him weakly. Her mouth was still covered with the life support equipment. So, she couldn't talk. Phil continued, "Now that the enemy of your soul Kevin O'Connor is no more, you can relax and breathe easy."

Ann smiled sadly. She remembered what she saw of Kevin in Hell and again felt plain sympathy for him. She chose to forgive them all right then and there. Just as the Lord had said, "You need to heal...". She thought let it begin now. The healing of her soul.

Phil continued, "You keep writing that nothing here is forever in your diary, but I want to tell you that everything good here on earth from now on will last for you at least this lifetime. I will make sure of that."

Boy was that prophetic, she thought. She closed her eyes and thanked God. Slowly she removed the equipment from her mouth as she spoke slowly,

"Phil... the tickets to India. It's...it's for the end of this week... I...."

"Were you planning to run away from me? Forget it in this lifetime at least. The Gomez's told me about it. I will cancel those and postpone them until after your delivery. I promise to take you there with your mother, Sue. Jade will be out by end of this month too."

He said his eyes were only concerned for her health. "And for now, just sleep Mrs. Jones. Rest. You need it. And so, does the baby. You will need all the energy for the upcoming wedding ceremony Elena will plan for you. I am marrying you twice to be doubly sure....and I love you, Ann Jones, like I have never loved anyone before." He said with all the mushiness he had forever avoided before this and kissed her forehead.

Ann smiled, "That much mushiness is so not you. Yes. I love you too, very much, Mr.... well Mr. Ogre Jones," she grinned.

He smiled and put his warm lips on hers banishing all her doubts and fears away. In her mind the poetry was ready,

So, this 'Cinderella' also rose out from the cinders, just like the one in the old story.
Her patience and her faith paying off even though her past was gory.
I always knew that love was all that I wanted in a world full of hatred and strife.
Now I know for sure that love is all that is needed to call my time on earth...Life.

THE END?
Not really

Author Bio

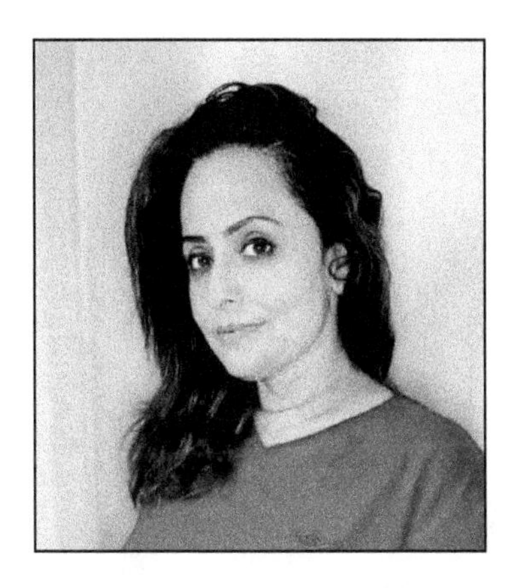

Vaishnavi MacDonald is a tv and film actress from Mumbai, India. She has already published her first book which is Autobiographical, *The Invisible Hand Of God*, on Amazon as paperback and on kindle.

She is blessed with so many things and writing is one of them. Her becoming an author has also been planned by God as she believes that she is totally a product of Grace.

Cinderella Effect.. Nothing Here is Forever is her first fiction book; a romantic thriller, based on the real, dark issues the title speaks of.

lotsa love

Vaishnavi

CPSIA information can be obtained
at www.ICGtesting.com
Printed in the USA
LVHW051443300321
682937LV00019B/975